SECOND CHANCE AT FIRST LOVE

PREQUEL

THE STORM BOYS SERIES

N.R. WALKER

COPYRIGHT

Cover Art: N.R. Walker
Editor: Boho Edits
Publisher: BlueHeart Press
Second Chance at First Love © 2023 N.R. Walker
Storm Boys Series © 2023 N.R. Walker

ALL RIGHTS RESERVED:

WARNING

TRADEMARKS:

BLURB

Paul Morgan has been running his luxury camping tour business in Kakadu National Park for the last five years. Taking small groups glamping, hiking, climbing, and swimming. It's been a busy five years, a hard five years, as he tried to forget the man he left behind.

Derek Grimes pushes people away—a self-preservation reflex. Because they can't break his heart if he breaks theirs first, right? Five years on, lost and lonely, he tracks down the one and only love of his life. Maybe seeing how Paul had moved on will help Derek move on too . . .

Paul can't believe it when a familiar name pops up on his client list, and Derek can't believe how good Paul looks, or just how happy living his dream job has made him. The spark between them never waned, but five years on, they've learned a few things about themselves and what they want.

They could have everything they ever dreamed of—if they're prepared to trust each other. Because a second chance at first love comes but once in a lifetime.

SECOND CHANCE AT FIRST LOVE

N. R. WALKER

THE STORM BOYS SERIES
PREQUEL

CHAPTER ONE
PAUL

I TIGHTENED THE RATCHET GRIP ON THE BACK OF my Cruiser and went back for the canisters of water. I'd done many five-day tours, taking groups of tourists from all walks of life out in the wilds of Kakadu National Park. It was my job, my business, and I loved it.

But I was nervous today.

I'd read the manifest, double checking all insurances and permits were in order. I was taking four individuals. Two women from Norway—both in their twenties, back-packing around Australia. One Australian woman in her fifties—an avid bushwalker, ticking Kakadu off her long list of conquests.

And Derek Grimes.

Thirty-three-year-old from Darwin, amateur astronomer.

My ex-boyfriend.

There could only be one Derek Grimes, thirty-three years old from Darwin who liked astronomy, right?

It had to be him.

It had to be.

Did he know I was running this tour specifically? That he'd be stuck with me for five days in the remote scrub of the tropical Top End?

Well, he was about to find out.

Instructions were to be at the meeting point in Darwin by seven am. From there, we'd drive out to the national park and do some sightseeing on the way. It was also so I could stock up and get essential supplies in Darwin before we left. And it was also the last stop of civilisation before venturing out into the vast, vast parklands. If they wanted a Coke or any kind of fast food, it was now or never.

We'd spend all of day one travelling, stopping to see the Mitsuaki Tanabe rock carving site, then on to the Mary River stop to see the crocodiles and have lunch. From there, I'd be taking them to my camp. It was a good hour off the main road, on a dirt track that was mostly inaccessible when the weather turned to shit. It was a solid first day of mostly touristy things, with a lot of hiking, and everyone was always glad to get to camp in time for dinner and an awesome sunset that only Kakadu could put on.

August was the dry season, which was peak tourist season. That didn't mean it never rained; it just meant it wasn't tropical monsoonal storms every afternoon.

And the next five days were supposed to be good weather. A bit of rain, not stinking hot and humid, but still hot for some. It was the Top End, after all. Most tourists underestimated just how hot and humid it got here, and what those kinds of temperatures did to the human body.

Some days were so bad, being locked in a sauna would be a reprieve.

But I loved it.

I loved the heat and humidity and the enormity of the most beautiful wilderness on Earth. I didn't even mind the mosquitoes, the wild water buffalo, the crocs, and other critters. But mostly, I loved the lack of people.

Even the limited crowds of Jabiru Visitor Centre in peak tourist season were enough for me. You can have your cities and rat races. Give me open space any day.

Give me anywhere where there is no chance of running into ex boyfriends who reminded me of how much I fucked up . . .

The first two of my client group turned up. Marit and Kari, backpackers from Norway. They both had long blond-ish hair plaited down their back, sun-kissed skin, wide blue eyes, and excited smiles. They'd been in Australia for five weeks and were loving every minute of it. They wore shorts and singlet tops, and I liked that they wore sensible walking shoes. Given they'd been back-packing for five weeks, they were well-accustomed to the Outback and Top End, and I was happy about that.

Next to arrive was Norah. With an H, as she was quick to remind me. She was fifty-six years old, from Sydney, and had done hiking trails all over the world. She came prepared, or so she said. Her backpack was expensive, but it looked well-used. She wore sensible hiking clothes and boots, which made me happy—I'd seen some ill-prepared and stupid people wear even stupider clothes out here—but she was already wiping sweat from her brow, and it wasn't even seven o'clock in the morning. And it was August, one of the milder months.

I'd have to keep an eye on her and make sure she stayed hydrated, for sure.

"Norah, this is Marit and Kari," I said, making introductions. They'd be spending the next five days together in the middle of nowhere, and I was glad they all seemed pleasant enough. I tapped my clipboard. "We're just waiting on one more."

The one I was both dreading and so very excited to see.

The one that had my stomach in knots . . .

"Oh, here comes someone," Marit said, nodding over my shoulder.

I turned around to see him walking toward us. He was carrying a duffle bag in one hand and a telescope case in the other. It was him, all right. God, he looked good. Still as handsome as ever. His dark hair was longer than it used to be, shaggy on top and was still damp. Just showered, maybe? The sleeveless shirt showed off his broad shoulders and defined biceps and a new tattoo. His chiselled jaw and his dark eyes . . .

Zeroed in on me.

Just short of reaching us, he stopped dead in his tracks. His duffle bag landed at his feet, fingers tightened on the handle of his telescope case. His jaw ticked. For a second, I thought he might have swallowed his tongue. "You?" he breathed.

"Nice to see you again too, Derek."

He sighed, looking back at the visitor centre, probably wondering if it was too late to cancel.

"Oh. You know each other?" Marit asked, her eyes wide.

I gave her a bright smile. "You could say that. It's been years though, right Derek?"

Derek mumbled something I didn't quite catch. It was probably just as well.

"Drop your bag at the tailgate," I said to him. "If you're still coming with us, that is."

He glared at me for a long second, and I wondered if he was about to bail. The tic in his jaw always gave him away. But he huffed as he brushed past me, and I had to bite back a smile. I made very quick introductions, and while they made small talk, I went to the back of the Cruiser to stack their bags. Resting my hands on the tailgate, I paused to catch my breath.

Derek.

The only man I'd ever loved.

Still as gorgeous as he had ever been.

This was going to be a very interesting five days.

Get it together, Paul. Be professional. What happened between you was a long time ago.

I could do this.

Easy as.

Right?

God, why did he have to look so good? Why did he have to smell all fresh-showered and have damp hair that hung into his eyes?

And why did he still have to look at me like he wanted to kill me?

Five days, Paul.

How bad could it be?

CHAPTER TWO
DEREK

I THOUGHT I WAS PREPARED.

I thought I was prepared to see him. I knew he was out here running these tours. I'd asked around. I'd stalked his social media. He'd made his dream come true, doing what he'd always wanted to do. I always knew he would. He was determined and driven.

And gorgeous.

And selfish.

The outdoor life seemed to serve him well. More rugged now, tanned, and with muscles that came from working hard. His light brown hair was short, his chest broad in his khaki uniform shirt, his thighs and calves thick down to his work boots.

I wasn't prepared for how good he'd look.

I wasn't prepared for the pang and stab of longing and regret.

And the anger.

I wasn't at all prepared for that.

But there he was, hot as hell with a smile I'd missed more than I'd realised.

He used to smile at me like that.

I was still in a bit of a daze as we all piled into his Cruiser. The crew-mover kind, fitted out like an army truck, or as if he was fully prepped for the zombie apocalypse.

"So how do you know each other?" Marit asked.

Her question struck me out of my thoughts and my gaze darted to Paul. I was sitting in the back opposite him, with a clear view of the side of his face. He had a small scar on his cheekbone that he hadn't had before . . .

I wonder how he got that.

When I hadn't answered, he did. "Ah, we used to work together in Darwin. A long time ago."

His eyes cut to mine in the rear-view mirror.

What he said wasn't a lie. We *had* worked together in Darwin years ago. That was how we'd met.

What he'd left out was that we'd also lived together. For two years. We'd met as co-workers at a bar and I'd needed to find a new place when my lease was up. He was looking for a roommate. We fell into stride with each other and then fell into bed.

But like he'd said, that was years ago.

I gave a nod. "Yeah, that sounds about right."

Sounded about wrong too, but whatever . . .

I checked my phone, noticing the bars of reception deplete the further we drove. Paul spoke most of the way, giving a sightseeing tour as we made our way deep into the park, first on tarred roads, then on dirt trails. Vegetation went from savannah woodlands to wetlands and then onto the lowlands. Towering rock walls, gigantic termite mounds, every tree and palm you could name. And Paul could name most of them.

First stop was the rock carvings, which were interesting and all, just not really what I was here for, but I was still glad to see it. It was good to see the three women enjoy themselves and, of course, getting to see Paul in his element.

I gave him some space, kinda hung back a bit.

He waited for me, a confused and uncertain look on his face and obviously decided to leave me alone.

Not that I could blame him.

The way we'd left things five years ago wasn't great.

Correction.

The way *I'd* left things five years ago wasn't great.

I didn't want to rush him. We had five days, after all, and I didn't want to ruin the whole thing on day one.

Next stop was the river cruise with the jumping crocodiles. I took a seat away from the edge of the boat, and after Paul got the two Norwegian girls and Norah—with an H, as she'd told everyone several times so far—settled in, he spoke to the staff on the boat for a few minutes. He clearly dealt with them regularly because they were all smiles.

He really had a whole new life now.

New business, new job, new friends.

New life.

New boyfriend, probably.

That twisted in my belly enough to make me feel

nauseous. What did I expect? What we'd had together was five years ago. Of course he would have moved on.

It's just you that can't move on, Derek.

I wasn't sure what coming out to see him was going to achieve. A stupid fairy tale reunion was a pitiful dream, I could see that now. So maybe at best, I could see with my own two eyes that he'd moved on and that I should do the same.

"You feeling okay? Lookin' a little pale. If you don't like boats, you should have said."

His voice was so familiar. I hadn't heard it in years, yet after just a few hours, it felt as if I'd never missed a day.

I'd missed him every day.

I let out a breath and glanced at him before nodding toward the front of the boat. "Nah, I'm okay." It wasn't like I could tell him the uneasy feeling was because I was imagining him having a new lover. "You do know that teaching crocodiles to jump out of the water for food isn't a good idea."

He grinned. "They tell people not to dangle over the sides and of course they never listen. Until they see the crocs jump up like that."

I shook my head. Stupid tourists. Actually, stupid tourism operators who thought of it. I pointed my chin to a group of people who were keeping clear of the edge. "Wanna bet they're locals?"

Paul chuckled, and with a sigh, his smile faded. "I saw your name on the group manifest. Wondered if it was you."

"The one and the same." I also wasn't about to tell him that I'd found out which tour operation he ran and chose it specifically so I could see him. So I lied instead. "Got a bit of a surprise seeing you."

He nudged me with his elbow. "I could tell by your face."

The shock on my face when I'd seen him had nothing to do with surprise. It was that he, after all these years, was standing right in front of me. Even more handsome than he ever had been.

Five years later, like an eternity and no time at all had passed.

"How've you been?" he asked.

"Okay," I replied. "Pretty good. How about you? Got your dream job, I see."

He flinched like my words had found their mark. I hadn't meant to sound so bitter. "Yeah. Been doing this for over four years now. I love it." He looked at me then. "What about you?"

I shrugged. "Much the same."

"Still at the bar?"

I snorted. "No. Office job. It's as bad as it sounds."

"But no nights and weekends or bar fights, right?"

I almost smiled. "Right."

He kinda smiled, and we watched the tourists marvel at the crocodiles for a while. "Still into the stars, I see," he said, giving me a smile. "Is that a new telescope?"

I nodded. He'd never really understood my fascination with the night sky. Hell, I didn't either, really. But he'd never thought it was weird or foolish like other people did, and I was still grateful for that. "Yeah. I've had it for about two years now. Someone said I needed to see the view from Kakadu." I shrugged again. "So here I am."

No one had told me to come to Kakadu. It was all my doing. Tracking him down, using it as an excuse to see him again. And, like he could see right through my bullshit, he stared at me for a long beat, his gaze searching mine. I don't know what he was looking for. The truth, probably.

"It's pretty spectacular," he said.

My pulse quickened—his effect on me still had a stronghold. Especially this close to me, where I could feel his body heat, smell his deodorant. Before I could form any words to speak, the crowd of idiots watching the crocodiles jump all squealed, and both Paul and I turned at the sound.

"Has anyone ever fallen in?" I asked.

"Not that I know of." He shot me a half-smile. "I did hear of a guy that needed to be choppered out of a canyon this year. Tried to take a selfie with a brown snake."

I snorted. "Play stupid games, win stupid prizes. You know, Darwinism is a thing."

He chuckled. "I try and instil a common-sense approach with my clients."

I nodded to the crowd. "Well, you better go have a chat with Norah with an H. She's about to get a fast-tracked membership to the left-handed society."

He looked over and, sure enough, there was Norah, first in line with the crocs. Paul sighed. "Ah, jeez." Then his eyes met mine again. "It's good to see you again, Derek."

Then he got up and went over to the crowd and I tried to catch my breath.

It hadn't gone terribly. In fact, it was a miracle he'd even spoken to me at all, so I was taking it as a win.

I still didn't know if he was seeing someone. Or hell, he could even be married for all I knew.

There was that sick feeling again.

Needing to distract myself, I got up and stood at the handrail. I figured if someone was going to lose a limb, then I'd want the best view possible.

CHAPTER THREE
PAUL

Derek hadn't changed much at all. He still had that dark gallows humour. He was still the brooding type, still a pessimist by nature, still pouty and still cute as hell.

I had so many questions to ask him.

He said he had an office job now, which didn't seem like him at all. But there was something else in his eyes. A resignation, a sadness. He'd always been a wallower. His glass was always half empty. That's just how he was.

He still had no tolerance for stupidity, and he never was a fan of people in general. But he'd always been insightful and thoughtful, and the few he let into his world, he treated like kings.

He didn't trust easily, and I'd thrown that back in his face.

Well, inadvertently. I hadn't meant to hurt him so much. But he'd trusted me, and I'd left him.

I could only imagine the wreckage I'd left behind.

He'd have put up more walls, maybe hated people a little more. And for that I was sorry.

He really was a wonderful guy—once you got past the prickles and barbs. I'd always said he was like a Bougainvillea: beautiful and sweet, thrived in the right conditions, but covered in thorns that would tear you to shreds with one wrong move.

He seemed even thornier now, and maybe that was my fault.

But still, it was so good to see him.

The crocodile cruise ended without any fatalities— thank god. We had some lunch where we got to know each other a little more. I got the feeling Marit spoke better English than Kari because she did most of the talking, and Norah became the mum of the group. She was nice enough, just had a very strong personality. Derek didn't say much and kept himself a safe distance from conversations. He wasn't rude, just happy to stick to his introverted self.

And we were soon back on the road, leaving the Arnhem Highway before we got to Jabiru and headed off-road. I gave the clients a bit of a guided tour, pointing out sights of interest and answering any questions.

My camp was a permanent campsite, with what one might call luxury or 'glamping' tents. They were technically eco-domes with solar power. Each had an elevated wooden floor, a camp bed or two, power outlets, and mesh walls that could open up to let in the breeze. They were spacious enough, had a small private bathroom each, and were decked out with fairy lights for ambience, with a small deck out the front to take in the spectacular view.

There was a common covered area where we'd do all

our cooking and eating and a fire pit for the cooler nights. The campsite was on top of a ridge looking out over the wetlands, which weren't too wet at this time of year. There were rocky escarpments to the right, quite a hike up to the top but worth it for the view. And there was a nice billabong and swimming hole further along the track to the left.

It was the perfect spot.

Not a soul for miles, which some people found a little worrying. I freaking loved it.

I had everyone grab their bags from the Cruiser with instructions. "Tent number one is a double so, Kari and Marit, that's you. Norah, you're in tent two. Derek, you're in tent three. I'm in tent four if you need me. There is always fresh fruit, crackers, and water in the communal kitchen. Help yourself at any time."

I gave them rules and instructions about safety and reminded them to never leave the camp without a backpack with water and emergency supplies. Even if they only intended to walk for five minutes. There was no room for mistakes out here.

None.

They all nodded and went off to their allocated tents. Giving them some time to get settled and freshen up usually gave me enough time to unpack the Cruiser. I plugged in the satellite phone to charge as I always did, and put the supplies away.

I found Derek standing at the edge of the campsite, looking out at the view. It was green wetlands to the horizon. Simply amazing. "Is this actually the Never Never?"

I almost laughed. Everyone knew that name from

Crocodile Dundee. "No. That part of the park is about a hundred kilometres southeast of here."

He nodded. "It's impressive. I can see why you like it here."

"You should see it in the wet season," I said. "Electrical storms all afternoon. The whole sky is a light show. The wetlands come to life. There's nothing like it."

His gaze cut to mine before he turned back to the view. "Can you get here in the wet season? I thought it'd be cut off."

"I live here," I admitted. "All year round. I spend very few nights away. The roads aren't great, and when the rains hit, there's very few visitors or tourists. Not up here where we are, anyway. The wetland tours still run. I do have a guy that comes this way in the wet season. He chases storms and studies them. Likes the lightning, apparently. Sometimes he'll stay here if the roads are impassable."

"He likes lightning? Is he insane?"

"No. He's a nice guy, actually. A bit of a wildcard, but you'd have to be to be setting metal equipment up in a lightning storm, right?"

His eyes flinched, hardening at the horizon. "Is he . . . are you . . . ?"

Am I . . . what?

He didn't finish the sentence, and before I could ask, Norah appeared by our sides. "Now, that's not exactly a terrible view," she said. "Any direct walking trails from here?"

Distracted by her question, I explained where the trails were, showing her which was best, longest, shortest etc, which of course just fuelled more questions. When I looked back, Derek was gone.

Is he . . . are you . . . ?

Was he trying to ask if the storm guy and I were a thing?

Tully Larson was a nice guy. Late twenties and yeah, maybe he was cute. But I had no idea if he could be interested because I had no intention of acting on it.

I hadn't acted on any impulses in a long time. I'd been busy, for one thing. Sure, I'd tried to have some one-nighters not long after Derek and I broke up. But they didn't feel right, just left me feeling hollow and empty, like I was trying to fill a void that could never be filled.

A Derek kind of void.

So I gave up trying after that. I hadn't looked at or touched anyone since.

"Tonight we'll be hiking up to the top of the escarpment," I told Norah. "It's not exactly arduous and I'm sure it'll be easy for you, but I promise you the view is worth it."

"I'm sure it'll be a walk in the park," she said, waiting for me to catch the pun. "Get it?"

I faked a laugh. "Oh yes, a nice and easy walk in the national park."

She preened a little, and she told me how she'd hiked the Overland in Tasmania last year. She'd also done Machu Picchu and had hiked some of the Appalachian Trail in North America as well as some walking trails in England along Hadrian's Wall, just to name a few.

It was remarkable, yes. And she certainly had some fascinating stories, which I was going to hear all about over the next five days, I was sure. But she was nice, if not a little preachy, and Marit and Kari were super friendly, and along with Derek, I was happy with the small group of clients. Everyone was amenable, pleasant enough.

But I really just wanted some alone time with Derek.

I wanted to talk to him, ask him about everything that he'd done these last five years, how everyone in his life was going, and what was the reason for the pools of sadness in his eyes.

"Who's up for a small hike to the top of the ridge?" I asked the group, pointing to the rocky outcrop that framed the righthand side of the campsite. "A picnic and a Kakadu sunset for our first night here. How does that sound?"

Everyone was in agreement, excited even. Except for Derek. He nodded and shrugged, but to use the word excited would be a stretch. "Sure," he said.

"Let's leave in thirty minutes," I said, making a point of checking my watch so they would too.

I packed some fruit salad, and cheese and crackers, and the plastic wine flutes that we could drink our juice or water from. And as we began our hike, I led the way with Norah behind me, then Marit and Kari, and Derek was last.

I hadn't planned it that way, but it actually worked well.

The escarpment had natural rocky steps, but the climb was vertical, and everyone had a backpack with their standard emergency water and supplies. Not heavy like an army kit but not light by any means. When I got to the top of the ridge, I helped pull each of them up the last step. The women were sweaty and puffing a little, and admittedly so was I. Derek seemed to be doing it easy, his biceps bulging as he pulled himself up. I held my hand out for the final step. He looked at my hand, then to my face, before he took my hand, somewhat begrudgingly.

His grip was strong and familiar, yet new all over again.

He dropped my hand first and brushed past me to join the others near the far edge, taking in the magnificent view. It was green national park for as far as the eye could see—to the horizon in all directions.

"Oh wow," Derek said.

Marit and Kari were grinning, taking photos, and Norah was already taking in landmarks for hiking and marking out where she wanted to go.

I set the blanket out and unpacked the picnic from my backpack. We sat around, eating the fruit and cheese, sipping juice, and watching the sky morph into vibrant pinks and oranges, then purples that had to be seen to be believed. It was almost other-worldly, and quite often the tourists who came here were first amazed but would often fall silent as the palette of soft colours washed over them.

I'd seen every single sunset and sunrise for four years, and they never got old.

They never would.

"I'd like to bring my telescope up here," Derek said. "Maybe tomorrow night." We were packing up and heading back down before it got too dark.

"We can come back later tonight," I suggested. If he'd wanted to come alone, well, that was out of the question. No one hiked alone out here. No exceptions. "But it's been a busy day. If you'd like to wait until tomorrow, that's fine."

"Oh." He baulked. "Uh, I just thought I could come back—"

"No one hikes solo," I said, offering my hand to Kari, who was going down the escarpment first. She smiled as she took the first step down, then Marit, and then Norah. They each took my offered hand and when it was Derek's turn, I held out my hand with a smirk.

He rolled his eyes and ignored me, taking the first step unassisted.

I would have been offended if I hadn't caught the hint of a smile.

"Tomorrow might be better," I said. It had been a long day, after all. "You can set up your telescope at camp tonight. Might be a good introduction," I said as we got to the bottom of the climb. "Then tomorrow night we can come back up here."

Derek gave a nod, not too pleased, but he didn't push, thankfully.

I went to the front of the line. I never let any guest dictate our schedule, so there'd be no arguing. And if I was being honest, as nice as some alone time with him on top of the ridge under the stars sounded, I wasn't sure I was ready for that. "I'll cook us some dinner first."

The plan was dinner and clean up, then we'd sit in the camping site in front of our tents, under the stars, looking out across the darkened valley below. I always lit a small campfire, not for the warmth but more for the experience. I boiled a billy of tea, like the Australian bushrangers used to do, and the clients loved it.

It was the perfect way to relax after a long day.

Kari and Marit were first to call it a night. They

thanked me for a wonderful first day and disappeared into their tent. Their lights went out shortly after.

Yet Norah stayed.

She was nice, I couldn't deny it. The strong personality type with opinions, but she was also smart and well-travelled, and normally I'd have enjoyed her stories. But my gaze kept drifting to Derek, who was basically ignoring us and looking up at the night sky.

I really just wanted some alone time with him, and the longer Norah talked, the longer the night dragged on, and the more I could feel my time running out. Like a clock was ticking down in my head, knowing my time with Derek was so limited . . .

"Oh, Derek," I said, as if I'd just remembered. "You might want to set up your telescope away from the campsite, away from the lights. Not too far though." I got up, effectively ending my conversation with Norah. "I'll grab the lantern."

Derek checked his watch. "It's a bit early," he said. "But I can already see so much out here."

"Wait until you get away from light pollution," I said, bringing the lantern out to him. "You wouldn't think a campsite would make much difference, but it does."

He smiled at me and my pulse quickened. The kind of carefree smile he used to have all those years ago. The one I saw in my memories, in my dreams . . .

"I'll just grab my backpack," Norah said.

Oh, great.

She was coming with us.

"Good idea," I said, aiming for a smile, even though it felt like a grimace.

"You're still a terrible liar." Derek was smirking at me. "Were you hoping for some alone time with me?" he murmured, but there was a glint of honesty in his eyes.

I hadn't realised just how much I was hoping for some alone time until it occurred to me that I wasn't getting it.

"Don't flatter yourself," I hissed at him.

He laughed, and my god, I'd missed that sound. But Norah was back before I could reply. She had her backpack on and her LED lantern in her hand. She was like a girl scout sponsored by a camping outlet. It was kinda fun. I showed her my lantern, which was like hers just ten times more powerful. "Are we ready?"

She nodded eagerly, and Derek rolled his eyes.

I led them to a cleared spot in the scrub I thought might be good. Just far enough away so the lights weren't a bother but close enough to hear if Marit or Kari needed me.

I set the lantern down while Derek set up his telescope. He'd always loved the stars and the vastness of space. Quite often I'd wake up to an empty bed and find him sitting in the backyard of the place we'd rented with his old telescope, his view looking ever upward.

I never thought to ask him what exactly he was looking for.

Or if he ever found it.

He used to say he'd just look at everything and nothing. I never questioned why he searched the skies. I just accepted that he did.

"Your new telescope looks pretty flash," I said as he set it up.

"Uh, thanks," he said. "I've still got the old one. But I can see more with this."

"Uh, Paul?" Norah said. "What wildlife is nocturnal out here?"

She was looking into the scrub, which was more of a wetland/lowland forest. There were trees, ferns, tall grasses, and a whole cacophony of wildlife that we couldn't see—but they could undoubtedly see us.

"There's a lot," I said. "Lots of mammals, frogs, lizards." I wasn't mentioning wild pigs and bats.

"Are there any crocodiles here?"

"I wouldn't have brought you here if there was," I said. "And I wouldn't be standing here."

She seemed to relax for a bit . . . until she thought of something else. She spun to me, her eyes wide, her face pale by the stark LED lantern. "Cassowaries?"

"You mean velociraptor turkeys with helmets?" Derek replied, not looking up from his telescope eyepiece.

I snorted but quickly reassured Norah. "No. There aren't any cassowaries here. And they're not nocturnal."

"But there are snakes and goannas," she added.

"This is Australia," Derek answered flatly. "So, yes. There is." He stood back from his telescope and gestured to Norah. "Take a look."

She wasn't as tall as him, so she had to pull it down a bit, but as soon as she put her eye to the eyepiece, she gasped. "Oh my god."

Derek grinned at me, and the warmth of it curled around my belly.

Norah looked up at Derek. "Is this for real?"

"Sure is."

She looked again for a few seconds, then stood back, wide eyed and excited, and let me have a look.

And holy shit.

I could see . . . everything. I could see it all.

So many stars. Countless. Bright and close, magnificent and unbelievable.

Like a disco ball or a snow globe or . . . There were no adequate metaphors.

"It's like nothing I've ever seen," I whispered. I turned back to Derek. "This telescope is way better than your last one."

"I know, right?" he said, taking the telescope again, putting his eye to the piece. "It's like a front-row seat on the Hubble."

I'd hate to think what his new telescope cost. "Did you get it from NASA?"

He chuckled. "Not quite." He was quiet then for a few moments. "It's even more breathtaking from here." He moved the telescope so he could pan across the Milky Way; he was looking for something, clearly. He grinned when he found it. "Oh wow."

He held it still and fixed the scope so it didn't move. "Here. Take a look at this."

Norah had another look and she gasped again. She was, quite surprisingly, speechless. She looked up at Derek, amazed. "Another first to add to my list," she said. "Of all the things I thought I'd see in Kakadu, Saturn wasn't one of them." She looked back through the scope. "I've never seen anything so beautiful."

My eyes drifted to Derek's. His longish hair fell to his

eyes, the muted lantern light catching all his features like a monochrome photo against the blackness around him.

I'd never seen anything so beautiful either.

"Here," Norah said. "Take a look."

Derek and I pretended we hadn't just been staring at each other. I put my eye to the eyepiece and looked.

And stopped breathing. What I was looking at literally stole my breath.

I glanced over at Derek, awe clear on my face. He smirked in return, like he'd known this secret all along.

"Jesus," I mumbled, looking back through the telescope.

It was Saturn and its rings in all its celestial glory. Like every high-definition photograph I'd ever seen, only better.

And with my own eyes.

"You look at these every night?"

When he didn't answer, I turned back to face him. He nodded. "Yeah."

"Derek," I whispered. "I'm . . ." I didn't know what I was. "Wow."

His smile was timid, personal somehow. And I wished we were alone. I wished Norah wanted to go back and it could be just me and him . . .

But instead, she began to tell me of the Northern Lights she'd seen in Iceland. She talked while Derek kept his eye to the telescope, and I kept my eyes on him. The way his jaw cut the dark night behind him, the column of his neck, how his long fingers handled the telescope with such care.

My mind took me back to our lives together. Him laughing in the shower, him moaning in my ear . . .

"Paul?" Norah asked, her voice cutting into some very private memories.

"Sorry? I was a million miles away."

"I just asked if you've ever seen the Southern Lights?"

"No. Not yet. Maybe one day."

Norah began telling me about the time she was in New Zealand, and I caught Derek's smile as he went back to looking through his telescope.

It wasn't long after that he began packing up.

"Did you want to stay?" I asked. "I can walk Norah back to camp and come back."

His eyes cut to mine. "Nah, it's okay. Been a long day."

So we walked back to camp. Barely fifty metres really, but it was through the scrub. When our tents came into view, my stomach began to tighten. Knots and butterflies, nerves and anticipation.

"Well, goodnight," Norah said, heading for her tent. "See you all bright and early."

Derek and I stopped. He glanced at his tent, then at me. For the longest moment, we stared at each other.

"Derek, I . . ."

"See you tomorrow," he said, turning and disappearing into his tent, the zippered door a finality in the silence.

I stood there for a second, trying to catch my breath. And it was only day one . . .

Yeah, we were definitely gonna have to talk.

CHAPTER FOUR
DEREK

CHRIST, THIS WAS A BAD IDEA.

When it was just me and him, the air between us crackled with tension. He had to be able to feel it. I wasn't imagining it. The way he looked at me, hot and familiar, but guarded now. Like he'd moved on and it was too late. Like he was sorry, but it was too late.

He'd mentioned the storm-chasing guy. The one who would come and stay with him.

I should have known he'd find someone new. I mean, Paul was a great guy. Handsome, funny, hard-working. He was running his own successful business. He was living his dream, and he'd never looked happier.

Who wouldn't want him?

I was pissed that Norah had joined us, but as I lay there staring at the tent ceiling, I was probably glad she had.

Because the second we were alone, Paul was about to tell me that it was good to see me, but . . . It was good to catch up, but . . . He was glad I was doing okay, but . . .

I didn't want to hear it.

My heart wasn't up for that.

Not on day one.

Day two wasn't shaping up to be much better.

We had a breakfast of bacon-and-egg sandwiches, coffee, and juice. Paul packed up our lunches, stacked everything into his Cruiser, and off we went again.

Our first stop was driving into the wetlands to a bird-watching spot, and it was pretty good. I wished I'd brought my smaller telescope from home, though there were binoculars for tourists to use. There was a flourish of different birds to see, and it wasn't even the wet season.

It wasn't what I'd come here to do, but it was interesting and good to see at least once. I liked listening to Paul talk about things he was passionate about.

It was a good reminder that he'd spent years learning his trade and that he was different to the Paul I used to know.

A good reminder, yes. Painful, but good.

After that, we drove along some bumpy path until the track basically ended with a turning circle and what was probably supposed to be a parking bay. "We walk from here," Paul said.

And walk we did.

It was a warm day and a touch humid, though Marit and Kari were sweating and flushed; Norah was red in the face. Paul kept an eye on her, and she kept saying she was fine; she just wasn't used to hiking in tropical climates. And that was probably true. Every place she'd talked about hiking before was colder.

"Don't worry about me," she said, drinking her water.

"If the elevation and steepness of Machu Picchu didn't kill me, Kakadu won't either."

Paul had laughed along with her, but I could tell he was keeping a close watch on her.

Paul and I were used to this climate, both being Darwin locals. In fact, it was pleasant weather for us. I was glad Norah hadn't chosen to visit in January.

The billabongs were beautiful, and I could see why they were popular. We hiked around to the far edge, and I wondered why Paul had suggested that when another group of tourists arrived soon after us. He'd definitely picked the best spot.

Marit and Kari went in the water first, laughing as they dived under. Norah gave me a nervous nod. "Are you going in?"

"Yeah. Guess I will," I said, dumping my backpack.

"There aren't crocodiles, are there?"

"Nah." Not the saltwater kind, anyway. I didn't say that out loud, even though it was right on the tip of my tongue.

Paul bit back a smile as if he could read my mind. "No, there are no crocs here," he said.

So, with a nod and seeing the tourists on the other side were also going in, Norah waded out into the water.

"Does she really think you'd bring them to a croc-infested waterhole?" I asked. "Anyway, she's more likely to meet an inland taipan here than a croc."

Paul snorted. "Don't say that."

I pulled off my socks and shoes and pulled my shirt over my head. Paul's gaze went straight to my chest, and I could tell he tried not to look, but the ink caught his eye.

"That's new."

It was a spray of pink, purple, and orange across my heart, with fine geometric lines in the shape of a trapezium.

I nodded. "So is the one on my back." I walked out into the water, giving him a full view of the new tattoo there. No one who ever saw it knew what it was, not without asking. It just looked like a large intersecting mass of triangles: fine lines, a geometric design.

A map of the stars, covering half my back.

Paul knew though.

He wouldn't know the significance, but he knew what they were at least. Probably the only person in my life who *would* know.

I dove into the water. Cool and refreshing, and exactly what I needed to clear my head. I swam out to where Kari and Marit were. Norah was floating on her back, drifting, looking up every so often to check where she was.

"Norah said your telescope is very good," Marit said. "She said we should look tonight. If that's okay?"

"Yeah, absolutely." The more people the better. It meant less chance of Paul and me being alone.

Coming here to see him had been a mistake. And even though it hurt and even though it was not the outcome I'd wanted, maybe I could use it as closure.

He'd moved on, and it was time for me to do the same.

Lunch was chicken and salad on bread rolls, with some cut fruit and juice. "Do you carry all this?" Kari asked, nodding. "Heavy to carry, yes?"

Her English wasn't perfect, but Paul was good at encouraging her to speak more often. He was so good at this job.

"Yeah, it's heavy," he agreed. "But it's good exercise. No need for a gym membership." He flexed his biceps with a grin. "And it's always lighter going back, which is the most important part."

My mind was still replaying his biceps flexing to realise that yes, he did have to carry all the food and drinks. Maybe that was why he insisted we each carry our own water, at least.

I kinda felt bad though.

The women decided on a short walk around the edge of the water to the rocky outcrop on the far side, but I was happy to sit in the shade. "I'll watch our camp," I said. "You guys go."

Paul studied me for a second. "Are you sure?"

I nodded, avoiding his eyes. He'd always been able to see right through me, and I didn't want him to see my truth right now. "Yeah. You go."

The three women were waiting for him, but with an unsure glance my way, he turned and met them on the path.

I watched as they disappeared into the scrub, and I sighed.

Dammit.

It was confusing, that was for sure. The way he'd look at me, or the way I'd catch him looking at me, was laced with a familiar heat. But then it was gone as quick as it had appeared.

The chemistry we'd always had was still there. The heat, the spark. The desire that saw us fall into bed far too easily. That connection had been missing from my life for five years, and it was back, itching under the surface the second I laid eyes on him.

But what good was it now?

If he did have another guy in his life, then all this anguish was for naught. But I needed to talk to him. I needed to clear the air, once and for all.

Only then would I be able to move on.

We got back to camp on dusk. Everyone had an hour or so before dinner, so I set my telescope up on the small porch in front of my tent. I could hear the low murmur of Marit and Kari talking. It wasn't in English so I could tune them out easily. And Norah was soon punching out some Zs in her tent.

Paul's tent was more of a luxury canvas cabin. It was still technically a non-permanent fixture, as I was certain permit restrictions insisted on in the national park, but it would take some more effort to remove his than the glamping tents. I could hear him moving around in his cabin, which I supposed was his home now. He lived out here, in the remote wilderness.

I didn't know if I thought he was crazy or if I envied him.

I was leaning toward the latter.

I envied the hell out of him.

Not wanting to travel down that lonely road, I looked through the eyepiece of my telescope and set my sights on things far, far away.

My memories betrayed me with something Paul had said to me years ago.

You're always focused on things so far out of reach, but you can't see what's right in front of you.

It was one of the last things he ever said to me. Before he left me. Before I pushed him away.

Those words haunted me still.

And maybe that was why I was here. To see what had been right in front of me.

To see what I'd lost.

Maybe part of me liked the pain . . .

"Whatcha looking at?" Paul's soft voice was right beside me. I hadn't heard him come over.

"Oh." I sat back. "Uh, just the moon."

"Just the moon," he repeated. "Nothing out of this world."

I almost smiled. "Was that a joke?"

He smirked, his eyes soft. "Can I see?"

I fixed the scope and gave him room so he could look. He was quiet for a second. "Jeez. You weren't kidding. That's like the actual fucking moon."

I snorted at that. "It is."

He was quiet for a second, his focus on the view in the telescope. "Why are you focused on that crater?"

"It's the *Mare Tranquillitatis*," I replied. "Or the Sea of Tranquillity."

Paul looked at me then. "That's a pretty name."

"It is. That's me, though. Still focused on things so far out of reach that I can't see what's right in front of me."

Paul's gaze flashed with recognition. With hurt.

"Yeah, look, Derek. I'm sorry."

"You don't need to apologise. You were right."

He turned to the view across the valley and sighed. "The same could be said about me. I was so focused on what was on the horizon, I didn't look at what was passing me by."

"But you're happy now," I asked, though it really wasn't a question.

"I mean, sure."

"With your storm guy?"

Paul's head turned so fast I thought I heard his neck crack. "What?"

"Oh, Paul," Marit said. "There you are. Can I ask you something? Do you mind? With the shower." She imitated turning the tap on. "The . . . handle. Is no water."

"Ah, yes," Paul said. "The tap. I know what you're going to ask." He stepped off my deck and headed toward her tent. "There's a valve . . . you have to be careful or there'll be a water fountain out of your sink."

They disappeared into her tent and I went back to looking at outer space. Past the moon, slowly zooming in on the unreachable stars. Things were so much easier up there. The emptiness, the vastness.

The silence.

Where things weren't complicated.

Where the loneliness didn't hurt.

DINNER WAS QUIET. Well, they all talked but I stuck to myself, like I usually did, and afterwards, Norah asked me if I was going stargazing again, up to the ridgeline like I'd mentioned the day before.

"Sure," I said. Then glanced to Paul. "If that's okay?"

I kept forgetting this was his business and I was a guest here. I needed to ask if it was okay first.

"Yeah," he said with a shrug. "Can't see why not."

"You two should come," Norah said to Marit and Kari. "The view through the telescope is amazing."

Oh goodie. Another group activity.

I repressed a sigh. I didn't mind them coming, I really didn't. I appreciated their enthusiasm for astronomy. It was nice that they were excited about it instead of rolling their eyes or mocking me, like some people did back home.

It was just something I normally did by myself.

It was always just me and the stars, the way I liked it.

It was personal and private.

Unless it was just me and Paul. I wouldn't have minded that.

But we were all going, apparently. And that was okay. I actually liked this group. There was no loudmouth, no raging extroverts that needed noise, or anyone who complained about every little thing.

I was grateful for that.

Sure, Norah liked to talk and tell her stories, but she wasn't overbearing. And when she started on her 'when I was trekking in Peru' stories, I could easily tune her out.

Like now.

We'd climbed up the escarpment, Paul had brought some picnic blankets and snacks, so while they sat around chatting, I set my telescope up.

I pretended it took a little longer than it really did, self-ishly taking in the night sky by myself while I had the chance. I zeroed in on Saturn again, given it was the perfect time of the year to see it from here. It was clear and bright and very beautiful.

"Kari? And Marit?" I gestured to the telescope. "Want to see something amazing?"

They came over, Marit looking first. She gasped and turned her wide eyes to me, then she looked back in the eyepiece. Then she let Kari have a turn, saying something to her in Norwegian, and Kari's excitement matched her friend's.

Then Norah had a turn, and Paul stood back, smiling. "Want to see?" I asked him.

His warm smile and soft eyes made my insides curl. "Maybe later."

Oh.

Was that . . . was that an invitation?

I wasn't sure.

"What is your favourite?" Marit asked. She waved her hand across the sky. "Of all the things."

"The Orion Nebula," I answered immediately.

I could feel Paul's gaze on me, but I avoided his eye contact at all costs.

"Can you show us?" she asked, her eyes as wide as her smile.

"Sure. It might take me a little while to get the focus right." I'd never looked at it from this exact spot before, after all. "Give me a few minutes?"

They went back to the picnic blankets, lit only by a few muted camping lanterns. The wind was picking up, a cool and welcome reprieve. And I put my eye back to the telescope and set my sights on the north-western sky.

"The Orion Nebula, huh?" Paul asked quietly. I hadn't

heard him come up beside me. He offered me a canister of water. I took it and had a sip. "The tattoo on your chest."

My eyes met his in the dark.

He recognised that?

"How did you know what it was?"

"I didn't. Not when I first saw it. But when you said it was your favourite." He shrugged, looking out into the vast darkness below. "I knew it was something star related. The purples and pinks, with the geometrical lines."

I held the eyepiece of my telescope. "Take a look," I murmured.

He stepped in close so he could look through the eyepiece. I didn't step back. I let him into my personal space, feeling the heat of his skin close to mine.

He looked at the nebula, then he looked at me. He glanced down to my chest, above my heart, to where the tattoo was under my shirt. "Your tattoo. It looks just like it," he whispered.

"It was born from a cataclysmic disaster. It has a black hole in its centre, holding it all together with a disproportionate gravitational pull. It pulls everything into its heart and decimates it." My voice hitched, so I swallowed so I could speak. "Like me."

He didn't say anything, but even I could see the sadness on his face in the dark.

I let out a slow breath, trying to steady my voice. "It's light-years away. Pretty to look at. Complex, misunderstood, and completely unreachable. And it's destroying itself." My nose burned with unshed tears. "Like me."

Paul shook his head. "Derek." He breathed my name, so soft and gentle it almost carried away on the breeze.

"I don't know why I came here," I admitted. "I missed you—"

"I'm not seeing anyone," he blurted out. "The storm guy isn't . . . I haven't . . . not since you."

I couldn't believe what I was hearing. I wasn't sure I'd heard him properly or even what he meant.

I shook my head. I didn't know whether to laugh or cry.

"Me either," I managed to say, my chin wobbling. I sucked back a breath and faced away from him. I wasn't any good at talking about feelings and shit. Never had been, which was the reason for this whole mess. "Fucking hell."

Paul's hand touched my arm. Firm, warm. Familiar. "We will talk," he murmured.

I nodded because that was all I was capable of doing. I noticed the girls were silent then and staring at us. "Found the nebula," I said, my voice stronger than I expected. I stepped back away from the telescope, away from Paul.

I needed some space and time to process what had just happened.

He wasn't seeing anyone. Hadn't seen anyone since me.

What did that mean? That he'd been too busy? Or that I'd left as big a hole in his life as he'd left in mine?

As the three women took it in turns to gasp and marvel, I practiced some measured breaths and even took a few sips of water.

Paul folded up the picnic blankets and stashed the food containers into his backpack. I walked over and handed him his water canister.

"Hey, just real quick," he said quietly. "When you said you shouldn't have come here, what did you mean? Cause it kinda sounded like you knew I'd be here."

Well, shit.

"Uh . . ."

He stood up straight and cinched the backpack drawstring. "Yeah." He pointed between us. "You and me? We're gonna talk."

CHAPTER FIVE

PAUL

I COULDN'T LET HIM DO THIS. HE WAS STILL THE same old Derek. Still gorgeous, still the brooding, sulking type, still closed off and still unable to talk about anything important.

Like emotions and feelings.

And the truth.

I couldn't let him derail every-fucking-thing again. Not like last time.

Did I blame him for our relationship imploding?

Not entirely. Because I was the one who'd walked away.

But his inability to talk about how he felt, what was troubling him, what hurt him, was a huge blinking neon fucking warning sign.

I knew he had his reasons not to trust people. I knew the stories about his fucked-up childhood and his fucked-up father, but what I didn't know was how to help him.

How was I supposed to help him when he refused to admit he needed saving?

Now here he was, five years later . . .

Here we both were. Five years had passed, yet we were both stuck grasping at dry sand. The harder you held on, the harder it was to hold.

I couldn't let him do this again.

It needed to be different. And it needed to be different from the get-go.

I didn't even know what we were or what our futures held. My life was here now. My business, my future. Where he fit into that, I had no clue.

We really needed to talk.

Which wasn't easy given the other clients were here, and I needed to be with them almost every waking minute of the day.

Which left night-time.

We never had any trouble *communicating* at night, if you know what I mean. When the lights went out and we found ourselves alone, our bodies communicated just fine.

That had never been an issue for us.

And maybe that was the problem. Maybe the sex was so good that we just forgot we had to talk like adults.

So that had to change as well.

No sex until we cleared the air.

If sex was even on Derek's agenda . . .

And from the way he was looking at me when we got back to camp, I was pretty sure it was. He was trying to catch my eye, trying to have a silent conversation in front of the others, trying to get a minute alone.

I took the food containers into the communal kitchen to wash up and he pretended to refold the picnic blankets. Norah was hanging out by the fire pit, so Derek kept his voice down. "Can I see you?" he murmured.

"When everyone's gone to bed. I can come to your tent . . ."

I turned to face him. "To talk. And talk only."

He winced but gave me a nod. "Yeah, of course."

"Can I help with anything?" Norah asked.

I gave her a warm smile. "Nope, all done. But thanks for the offer. I'll be heading to bed shortly, so it'll be lights out soon." I checked my watch. "Say ten? We've got another early start tomorrow."

Those instructions were more for Derek, and with a glance at him as I walked away, he gave me another nod.

I cleaned up my cabin, not that anything was too messy, but living in such small quarters, everything had to be in its place. I scrubbed my face and brushed my teeth, then changed into my pyjama bottoms and shirt. They were kind of hokey, given they were old-man PJs with my company logo monogrammed on the breast.

I waited for Norah's light to go out, then Derek's, knowing he wouldn't be far away.

My belly was full of butterflies and slippery knots. A small part of me wanted him to not show up, but a larger part of me was just about beside myself so when there was a gentle rap on the door, I almost jumped out of my own skin.

I opened the door, and Derek's pale silhouette in the moonlight made him look hauntingly beautiful.

I stood aside and he came in, not sure whether to sit or stand. He wiped his hands on his thighs and licked his lips.

"Take a seat," I said, gesturing to the sofa. I pulled the

seat at my table out for me, figuring the distance—as small as it was—would do us good.

He sat and let out a long, steady breath. I was expecting him to not speak or to offer very little, like he used to do. But he just started to talk and, like a dam where the weight of the water was too much to bear, the wall cracked and the words spilled out.

"I knew you were here," he said. He spoke to the floor, to his fidgeting hands. "I kept track of your social media. I followed the leads and found your business here. Sounds creepy. I'm sorry. But I had to know you were okay, and I knew you didn't want to talk to me. It wasn't like I could have called . . ."

"You could have," I whispered.

He flinched and he took an unsteady breath. "I haven't been doing too good since you left." His chin wobbled a bit, but I knew he needed to say this. He needed to get this out. "I mean, I wasn't doing too good before you left either, and I know I fucked up. I pushed you away. I push everyone away. It's what I do, and I'm trying to not do that anymore." He grimaced. "I got a job in an office. I hate it, but it pays the bills. It's stifling and soul-crushing, and every day I dream of leaving. I envy you for doing what you always dreamed of doing. I know I told you that you were foolish." He shook his head. "I was scared of losing you, and I lost you anyway. You couldn't be the one to leave *me* if I pushed you away. I should have encouraged you to do this. I should have told you how proud I was of you." His breath trembled and his eyes met mine. Glassy, wet, vulnerable. "I'm so sorry for everything I said. For everything I did to hurt you. I don't know why I came here. I needed to see you. I thought maybe if I did see you, you'd either tell me to fuck off or I'd see how you'd moved on without me, and maybe then I could finally move on too."

He shook his head and a tear fell down his cheek.

"But I . . ." Derek swallowed hard and put his hand up, like he needed a minute. He recomposed himself. "This isn't easy for me. Nothing like this is easy for me. I can't talk about this shit. But I'm trying, Paul. I'm trying."

"I can see that," I said, unable to speak above a whisper. I wanted to touch him, to hold his hand. But he needed to say this, and frankly, I needed to hear it. "Take your time."

He nodded. "I thought if I came here and saw that you were happy, that maybe you had a new boyfriend, that it'd be the closure I needed. Because I've been stuck. I can't move on. Not from you or from what we had. From what I threw away. I've been so lost. I didn't know what else to do." He put his hand to his heart. "But then I came here, and I saw you. And you looked at me and you smiled."

Another tear fell down his face. He wiped it away.

"Maybe it'd be easier if you hated me," he said, crying now. "I could understand that. I could deal with that." Then he shrugged. "I would deserve that."

"No you wouldn't," I murmured. "Derek, what happened between us was not your fault. We both threw it away."

"I shouldn't have said what I did."

"And I shouldn't have either," I countered. "We were young and hurting. Our lives were changing, and we didn't know how to deal with that. I don't hate you. I could never hate you."

His gaze cut to mine. "You don't?"

I shook my head. "Never." I took a deep breath, now it was my turn to talk. "I wanted to start my own company. I saved money, I studied business. I had plans. You knew that. We talked about it all the time."

He nodded.

"It didn't have to mean the end of us. It just meant things would change, and that scared the shit outta you."

He nodded, another tear falling.

"I'm trying to be better. I want to be better."

"It's not a terrible flaw," I said quietly. "I knew you. I knew you were freaking out and all those horrible things you said were just barbs you put up to protect yourself."

His face crumpled and he began to cry. "I'm so sorry."

"I'm sorry too, Derek. But it's not all your fault. I could have tried harder too. I could have told you to pull your head out of your arse. I could have dragged you out here. You would have bitched and complained, but you would have done it. And it would have been hard. And we would have struggled in the early days. It wasn't easy. Hell, it's still not. But we would have done it."

He looked at me, confused. Which was probably fair, because I didn't even know what I was saying.

"We both could have tried harder," I said. "And I'm sorry we didn't."

He nodded then. "Me too."

We were quiet for a moment, letting the dust of our pasts settle around us.

He spoke first. "I haven't dated anyone else. I haven't

even looked. I just couldn't. I never got over you. In my mind, you were this perfect time of my life that nothing will ever compare to." He managed a sad smile. "Kinda like looking at a galaxy that died a million years ago, but we can still see it because the light hasn't reached us yet. In hindsight, it's spectacular and brilliant. But in reality, in real-time"—his chin wobbled again—"it's no longer there."

God, his words . . . he'd always had a poetic way with words.

I ached to touch him, and against my better judgement, I went and sat beside him and took his hand. It was warm and strong, familiar yet new. "We can't change what happened. The words we said, the heartache. What's done is done. But I'm glad you're here. I'm glad we can talk about what happened. For both our sakes. For us to both move on."

"I don't want to move on," he whispered, his hold on my hand tightening. "I want to go back."

"But we can't. We're not those two guys anymore."

He shook his head, eyes welling with more tears. "What are you saying?"

"Derek, we're not those two young kids anymore. We worked nights behind a bar and dreamed during the day. We were so in love. We were reckless with it. We had something so wonderful, but we didn't understand just what we had. And that's exactly what young love is. What a first love is."

"My only love," he mumbled.

His words hurt me. The look of sadness on his face hurt me.

"Mine too. I've never loved anyone else. Not before, not since." I held his hands in both of mine. "I wish I knew the answers. I wish I knew how to fix this. But I don't know what you want, and I don't know what I can offer. But Derek, we can't go back. We can't go back to how we used to be, because it would just all end the same."

He was staring at that in between space. At the floor, at his memories, I wasn't sure. He pulled his hand away and swallowed hard. "I get it. I do. I understand. Thank you," he mumbled. "For talking tonight. It was good to clear the air. And maybe now I can move on."

Wait a minute . . .

"Derek, stop," I said, maybe a little more harshly than I'd intended.

His gaze darted to mine, but he recoiled a little.

This right here. This right here, where he assumes the worst, shuts up like a clam and withdraws into himself . . . ugh. Frustrating as hell.

But he was trying.

And he did say what was on his mind earlier, and he'd said it well. Even though it was hard for him.

I could see he was trying.

"Derek, what do you want?" I asked. "Tell me right now. What did you come here for? Give me your best-case scenario."

He shook his head. "I don't know. I just don't know. I wanted . . ." He licked his lips and tried again. "I wanted you to not hate me. I wanted you to forgive me. To tell me it was okay. To tell me you . . ."

"To tell you what?"

He winced again, but man, my emotions were running

high, my patience was worn thin. "You wanted me to tell you what, Derek? Enough of the not-saying-shit out loud. We're not kids anymore. So no more childish games. We're adults." Goddammit. I was mad now, and I tried to keep my voice down. "We need to be able to say shit out loud. So tell me. What did you want me to tell you?"

"I wanted you to tell me you still loved me!"

His outburst was made louder by the silence that followed. He sucked back a breath that was a half sob. "I wanted you to tell me you never moved on. Like I hadn't. I wanted you to tell me there was a hole in your life like there was in mine. I wanted you to tell me you still loved me because I'm still in love with you. I tried not to be, and I thought I'd just made up this illusion of who you were, like you were some perfect guy, and I hoped I'd get here and realise it wasn't true. You couldn't possibly be as perfect as I remembered, but then I get here and . . ." He waved his hand at me, up and down. "You're more perfect than I remember."

Oh wow.

Okay. I wasn't expecting the L word . . . considering he couldn't even tell me that when we were together.

"And it's made everything so much worse," he added quietly. "Because now I know. Now I know that you are everything I need, but it's too late." He let his head fall back, blinking and trying to breathe through his tears. "I'm sorry. I'm not used to saying this shit out loud. God, it hurts."

I tried to steady my breaths. My heart was hammering, aching.

I hadn't expected this. I hadn't expected him to turn up

at all. Least of all pouring his heart out to me in ways he'd never been able to before. I hadn't expected him to still love me.

I hadn't expected to welcome hearing it. It made me happy. Cautiously, maybe even sceptically. But happy, nonetheless.

"Do you think you could get used to saying it?" I asked, threading his fingers with mine.

He looked at me, confusion mixed with hope in his dark eyes. "What?"

"I don't know what the answers are, Derek. But seeing you here . . ." I shook my head slowly. "You're as beautiful as you ever were. As poetically tortured as you ever were."

He made a face, half-smile, half twisted pain.

"You were my first love," I admitted quietly. "I never got over you. I thought of you often. Wondered what you were doing, if you'd moved on."

He shook his head again. "I couldn't."

"Me either."

His gaze fixed on mine. "Paul?"

"I'm not saying yes. I'm not saying I know what any of this means, because I don't. But I'm so fucking glad you're here. It's stirred up a lot of memories and emotions and I'm not sure what to make of it." And that was the honest truth. "But it's not a no. I don't know what it is. But I'm interested in finding out."

He looked at me, eyes wide, disbelieving, and full of tears. "Do you mean that?"

I nodded. "There's gonna be some terms and conditions. Like a whole fucking list. And we're going to start with talking. Actual conversations about what we want and what we expect."

He nodded, but another tear escaped down his cheek. "I just want to be with you. In whatever capacity, whatever it takes." He wiped his cheek with the back of his hand. "I've never known peace except when I'm with you."

Oh man.

My heart ached for him. I put my hand to his cheek. "Derek, your peace needs to come from here," I said, sliding my hand down to press against his chest.

He frowned, his whole face a mask of sadness. "I know. But it's easier when I'm with you. Just being near you makes it easier."

I wanted to kiss him. I so badly wanted to press my lips to his, to take even the smallest of his burdens. But we weren't there yet.

His eyes searched mine, as if he was looking for permission.

I took his hand, and holding it in both of mine, I moved an inch or two away, our legs no longer touching. "I don't want to fall into bad habits. It'd be so easy to just fall back into bed, but then we'd never talk about anything. And there's a lot we need to sort out."

He nodded, and he even smiled a little. "I want to tell you everything, but there isn't much to say. I've been treading water since you left. Barely keeping my head above the surface."

"Was coming to see me like a sink or swim type of thing?"

Derek's gaze met mine, intense and honest. He nodded. "Exactly like that. I had to try and move on, except I didn't know how. I thought if I could just see you . . . If you weren't as perfect as my memories made you out to be, or if you were with someone new." He shrugged. "But there you were, still the same, but different. Hotter than you were. Not sure how that was possible cause you were always pretty fucking hot."

I snorted out a laugh. "Thanks."

"But you were happy," he continued, smiling at me. "You were that ray of sunshine that had been missing. I've had nothing but gloomy skies and . . . grey. Everything's been so grey. And you . . ." He searched my face. "You stood there by your Cruiser in your sexy Steve Irwin outfit like a ray of fucking sunshine."

I chuckled. "Steve Irwin?"

"The khakis," he replied. "I like them, don't get me wrong. Not sure on the PJs though."

I looked down at my clothes. "Hey, these are my professional pyjamas. When I first started, a storm came through in the middle of the night and took a branch down near tent one. There was an almighty crack and someone screamed. I ran out wearing some boxer briefs. And not a stitch more. Needless to say, the next day, I ordered some professional pyjamas online. That way, if I have to run out in the middle of the night, I'm wearing something a little more professional."

"I'd prefer the boxer briefs," he murmured.

I knew that look he was giving me.

I cleared my throat and squeezed his hand. "And this is why we need to talk. As much as I want to kiss you right now—" I shook my head. "—I don't want to make the same old mistakes."

He looked at the floor again and chewed on his bottom lip for a while. "What do you want to know? I'll tell you everything. I've pretty much recapped the last five years. I did nothing. I saw no one. My dad's back in jail again, so that's something new, I guess. Well, not new. But you know what I mean. I rent a one bedder in the city. It's okay, nothing flash."

I didn't really mean that kind of stuff, but I was glad he told me. "Sorry about your dad."

"I'm not."

I wasn't either.

"I've got some money saved," he said with a shrug. "I don't go out and I don't drink, so whatever I earn just sits in my account. I bought the new telescope. And that's it. There's nothing else to tell. I wasn't lying when I said I was stuck, Paul. I'm just . . . stuck. Treading water, getting nowhere."

I took a deep breath and exhaled slowly. "And what do you want to do now?"

His gaze cut to mine. "I want to be with you."

"But how?"

"I don't know."

"Where will you live? What about your job? Your unit in Darwin?"

Derek shook his head. "I don't know," he whispered.

"Are you even talking about dating again? Or just friends?"

"I don't know," he said, more desperate this time. "What I want is you. What we had. Boyfriends, lovers, living together. I would kill for that. But I'll take whatever I can get. And that sounds pitiful, I know, but you know what? That's where I'm at. I needed to tell you that I'm sorry, and to beg and grovel if I had to."

Letting go of his hand, I brushed a strand of hair off his forehead. "You don't need to beg. I'm glad you're here. I meant it when I said that. I'm sorry for how things ended with us too. We were just young and pigheaded, and too proud to admit what we needed. But we're older now. I'd like to think we know better."

He nodded quickly, but there was a hint of fear and uncertainty in his eyes. "I don't know how to make it work, like you said. Logistically, I have no clue. I didn't come here with a plan. To be honest, I was expecting you to laugh at me and tell me to fuck off."

I nudged my shoulder to his and chuckled. "I was just glad it was you and not some other Derek Grimes on my guest manifest. I wanted it to be you."

His eyes searched mine, a smile pulling at the corner of his lips.

"And you're willing to figure it out? For real?"

"I am."

His smile was breathtaking.

"But," I cautioned, "things will be different this time. They have to be."

He nodded. "I know."

Then he looked at my mouth, and he licked his lips.

I laughed and stood up. "Uh, yeah." I walked to the door and let out a loud breath. "I think I mentioned taking things slow a few times, and you looking at me like that doesn't help."

With his hands on his knees he stood up slowly, a smirk on his lips. "Looking at you how?"

"You know damn well." I opened the door for him. "Goodnight, Derek."

He pouted, but it was playful and shy. He walked to the door, standing closer to me than he had to. "Goodnight," he murmured, his voice low and rough.

I grabbed his arm, stopping him from leaving. I pulled him closer, our bodies pressing together. I looked at his lips, at his beautiful, smirking lips, then at his eyes. They were dark and swirling with familiar heat and pleading.

And all the permission I needed.

I slid my hand around the back of his neck and pulled him in for a kiss. It was hard stubble and soft lips, open and teasing, but no tongue, no tasting.

He grunted, and when I pulled back and put some distance between us, he whined.

"See you in the morning," I said, my voice betraying me.

He put his hand to my chest. Surely he could feel my heart thumping against my sternum, and from his smile, maybe he did. "Thank you, Paul."

THE NEXT MORNING, I was running a little later than I'd have liked. I'd barely slept. My mind kept replaying the kiss, his eyes, his smile.

It was a physical and emotional effort to have him leave my cabin last night. But it had been the right thing to do.

As much as my body disagreed, my heart and my brain were in charge this time.

Breakfast was a bit rushed, not that Marit or Kari noticed, and Norah didn't seem to, either. But Derek slipped into the communal kitchen and came to the sink, shoving his hands into the water and bumping me out of the way. "I'll finish washing up," he said. "You seem a bit frazzled this morning."

I would have growled at him if he wasn't right. In fact, I appreciated his help. "I was a bit slow out of bed this morning," I admitted. "Didn't sleep too well."

His gaze shot to mine. "Oh? In a good or bad way? Not like a having-second-thoughts lack of sleep."

"No." I ignored the heat in my cheeks. "More of a couldn't-get-someone-off-my-mind kind."

He raised an eyebrow, smiling, just as Marit came in. "Can I help with anything?"

"No, it's okay," I said quickly. "I was just about to load up the Cruiser."

"Oh, I can help with that." She decided she was helping whether I liked it or not. So I had her help me, and soon enough we were on the road for our day's adventure.

It was a lot of hiking, and though it was mostly flat, it was still humid. Getting close, you could hear the water-falls and the river, and it ramped up the excitement. As soon as everyone walked through to the clearing and saw the amazing scenery, they soon forgot about how long and hot the hike was. The waterfalls made it worth it though.

It was one of my favourite spots.

Derek seemed to smile a bit more today, and he hung around me more. He even helped me carry stuff.

He also waded out into the water with Norah for one final dip before heading back. The walk back to the Cruiser was never as much fun as the walk to the waterfalls. Everyone was tired, the late afternoon sun was hot, the air getting humid.

A storm was rolling in across Kakadu. Not like the summer electrical storms, but the clouds were dark, the air thick.

When we got back to camp, everyone opted to freshen up with a cool shower, so I pulled out the camping chairs and sat them at the edge of the drop off. I served up some cheeses and crackers with grapes and juice, and I deliberately put Derek's telescope next to my chair so he'd sit next to me. When he walked out, he saw it and smiled at me in a way that made my heart knock against my ribs.

His damp dark hair hung in his eyes, his tanned skin the colour of honey in the stormy sunset.

I wanted to drag my teeth across the back of his neck. I wanted to taste his skin, see if it was as delicious as he smelled . . .

"Yeah, of course," Derek said. I realised then that my mind had been in the gutter and I'd missed the conversation. He took out his telescope and set the sights across the horizon, then they all took it in turns looking at the trees and wetlands that carpeted the scene before us.

The storm rolled in over the horizon, dark clouds of purple and orange with sparkling pockets of lightning and we could smell the downpours of rain in the distance.

It was an incredible sight.

It was a magical moment.

I cooked our BBQ dinner, and the five of us stayed there in our camping chairs watching over the world until long after the sun had set.

Derek shared his telescope around and his knowledge of the stars above us until Norah went to bed first, followed soon after by Marit and Kari.

"So, it's just us," he whispered.

"It appears so."

He sighed. "It's easy to see why you live here. This," he murmured, nodding to the darkness that now lay out before us. Then he gestured to the camp. "And this?"

"It's pretty amazing, isn't it?"

"Yeah."

He was quiet again for a while. Some crickets chirped and a hawk cried somewhere not too far away. He turned his gaze to me, a peaceful smile on his face. "You asked me what I wanted. Just this; you and me, and nothing else. That's what I want."

It was a nice dream.

But reality and finances would probably disagree.

He seemed to read my mind. "I don't know how to make it happen. But this is what I want."

I reached out and squeezed his hand. "If you want it bad enough, you'll find a way."

"Yeah, okay," he said, getting up. "I'm turning in. I'll see you in the morning."

It was so abrupt and curt, I was taken by surprise. "Yeah, okay," I said to his back. He was halfway to his tent already.

He jumped up onto his deck, opened the door, and stopped. "Ah, Paul?" he yelled.

I was up and out of my chair and right behind him in a second. My first thought was a snake . . .

He had water pouring out of his bathroom and onto his bed.

I dashed in and shut the water off. The shower valve had been shut off, and the basin spout had very deliberately been turned at the perfect angle to spray his bed.

I shot him a dirty stare. "Derek?"

"Oh no," he said flatly. "My bed's all wet. Looks like I'll need to sleep in someone else's bed . . ." He shrugged. "Say, in yours, perhaps?"

CHAPTER SIX

DEREK

Did I sabotage my bed? Yes.

Was I sorry?

Not one bit.

Paul was kinda mad, and I should have felt bad about that, but I threw my bag down on the floor of his bedroom and grinned at him. "Oh no. There's only one bed."

He was trying not to smile. "You did that deliberately."

"I don't know what you're talking about."

He raised one eyebrow. "Derek."

"You said I needed to action a plan. So I did. You said I needed to be more honest about what I want and how I feel. So I was."

"With words."

"We're talking, aren't we?"

He sighed and ran his hand through his hair. "I should make you sleep on the couch."

I looked at the couch. "I mean, I will if you want me to . . ." Then I looked at him. "But you don't want me to.

The way you kissed me last night . . . I had to do something."

His gaze narrowed, trying to be mad at me, but when I laughed, he rolled his eyes and sighed. "We still need to talk."

"So let's talk. In bed."

He rolled his eyes again. "Derek, we—"

"I mean it. Talk only. I don't want you to be mad at me for doing what I did, but we have limited alone time together, and I don't want to leave here in a few days with things left undone."

He stared at me. "You really just want to talk?"

"Yes. If that's what we need to do, then yes."

He was sceptical, or probably flat out didn't believe me, and I couldn't blame him. Our sex life before had always been hot and electric, and I was usually the one to instigate it. Sex was easier than dealing with responsibilities and emotions and shit.

This time would be different.

It had to be.

"If I'm getting a second chance," I said quietly, "then I'll do anything in my power to not fuck it up. I meant what I said before, Paul. I'm serious about trying to do this right."

"And you call coercing yourself into my bed the right thing to do?"

I pulled my shirt over my head. "I said I was trying to do the right thing. But I'm still me."

He ogled my chest for a bit, then snapped out of it. He snatched up his pyjamas, went into his bathroom, and closed the door. When he came out, I was in his bed. "I take it from the book on your bedside you still sleep on the right side of the bed."

He tried to glare at me, but with another long sigh, he walked to his side and pulled back the cover. "I'm still mad at you."

I snuggled down and, facing him, folded my arm under my head and smiled. "You're still sexy when you're mad."

He ignored that, turned the lights off, got into bed, and pulled the covers up to his waist. He stared at the ceiling for a few moments, then turned onto his side to face me. "Your hair's longer."

"Not deliberate," I said with a shrug. "Just kinda stopped caring about a lot of things."

He reached over, and with the gentlest of touches, he brushed a strand of hair from my eyes. "I like it," he murmured. "And the tattoos."

I studied his eyes and, even in the dark, I could see honesty staring back at me. Sure, it was hard to say this stuff out loud, but I could trust him. I'd always been able to trust him. And I was safe with him. "I've been trying to fill the void, ya know? Trying to find something to fill the hole in my life. Tattoos seemed like a good idea. I love the ones I have, but . . ." I sighed. "The fix was only temporary."

He slid his hand over mine. "I'm sorry you had it tough."

"Did you?" It was a stupid question to ask, but I had to know. "Did you struggle at all?"

"Of course I did. I was heartbroken. I was busy, which helped. And I loved that I could channel my energy into getting this all set up. It took a while . . ." He frowned. "The nights were the worst. Lonely, and the quiet and remoteness made me wonder if you were right. If I was crazy for throwing everything away and chasing a dream."

I flinched. "I'm sorry I said that. And you know it wasn't true." I threaded our fingers. "I was just scared, to put it bluntly. You wanted to move on and leave me behind. I just needed to hurt you like I was hurting. It was childish, and I regret every word I said."

"I never wanted to leave you behind. I asked you to come with me. My plan was for you and me to do this." His lip pulled down. "But you didn't want it."

I let go of his hand and rolled onto my back. Telling this to the ceiling instead of looking into his eyes was so much easier. "I was scared. I was scared of change. I was scared of the unknown. Of failure. And you know why. Growing up with my dad . . . my entire life was an unknown." I swallowed down the lump in my throat. "And then I met you, and I had the first permanent things in my life. A job, food, a house."

"Hey," Paul said, reaching over for my hand again. "Look at me."

He waited for my eyes to meet his.

"I know. It's why I never blamed you." He shook his head, sadness etched on his face. Even the darkness couldn't hide it. "I blamed me. I fucked it up because I didn't try hard enough. I should have fought harder to show you, to prove to you."

I rolled back onto my side to face him properly, our knees bumping. "It wasn't your fault."

He sighed. "No. It wasn't yours either. We were just young, like I said. That's all. We didn't know how to handle it. We didn't talk enough. I should have told you every day that I loved you, that you were worth it."

Tears burned in my eyes. "I should have . . . I didn't . . ." I let out a shuddered breath. "I should have told you too."

He smiled, the silver moonlight outlining his face. "It's not too late for us. Seeing you again, having you here with me, it's like no time has passed at all, Derek. And I'd be lying if I said that didn't scare the shit outta me."

"I want it to be like it was. I want that with you," I whispered. "But you're right. Things need to be different this time. I need to be better this time. At saying shit out loud."

He chuckled warmly. Sleepily. "And I need to be better too." He put his hand to my cheek. His rough, warm hand felt divine. He stroked my cheek with his thumb, then pulled me in for a soft kiss. "Goodnight, Derek."

"Night, Paul. I'm not sorry about my bed."

He didn't open his eyes, but he did smile.

And I watched him sleep. Almost scared to close my eyes in case this was all some stupid dream.

Could it have been this easy?

It wasn't easy, Derek. You warred with yourself for a year about doing this. You struggled every minute of every day.

But he said he wants me back. Just like that.

Yeah, funny what happens when you decide to be a grownup and tell him how you feel.

I sighed, knowing there was no point in arguing with myself anymore. Overthinking and closing in on myself to shut everything else out had got me through most of my childhood. And it had served me well. But that was before

Paul. That was before finding true love, finding someone who thinks I'm worth their time.

I didn't need to protect myself anymore.

I had to open myself up, as scary as that might be, and let him in.

Properly this time.

Forever this time.

Watching him, studying the lines of his face in the dark, I knew he was sound asleep. So I snuggled in a bit closer, and closer still, until his arm slid around me and pulled me close. With my head on his chest, his arms around me, it was the safest I'd felt in years.

I smiled into his neck and closed my eyes and breathed him in.

I slept like a baby.

I WOKE up to a smack on the arse. "You gotta get up," Paul said.

I opened one eye. He was showered and dressed, and I was spread out in his bed, hugging his pillow instead of him. I whined. "Mmm."

"The others will be awake soon. I'm starting breakfast early. We've got a busy day today."

I groaned again, rolled over, and kicked back the sheet. His gaze went straight to my morning wood. He grunted, and I chuckled, still half asleep. "Don't blame me. I was having a very good dream and hugging your pillow that smells a lot like you."

He seemed stuck for a second, like his brain was

glitching out. He wanted to stay but he knew he had to walk away. "I'll be . . . cooking breakfast."

"I'll be jerking off in your shower."

He tripped over his own feet, stumbled through the doorway but kept walking, grumbling as he went.

I chuckled and rolled out of bed.

In all seriousness, he did have a job to do. And also, in all seriousness, I did jerk off in his shower, imagining my hand and the warm, soapy water were his mouth. It only took a few strokes and a very vivid imagination, a replay of some of my favourite memories, and remembering his arms around me last night.

It was a pretty quick shower.

I got dressed, hoping to slip out of his tent unnoticed. I took one step out of the door and Marit and Kari both stopped dead on their way to the communal kitchen. Kari nudged Marit, and Marit smiled as if her suspicions proved correct.

"Morning," I said brightly. Then I yelled out to Paul. "I, uh, I couldn't find the . . . thing."

Paul looked up from the hotplate. "What?" Then, seeing the two girls, he shot me a wild look, his face a shade of red. "Oh. Okay. Uh, thanks."

We were terrible actors.

I made a beeline for my tent to avoid any awkward conversations, and to also assess the damage.

It wasn't so bad. Just a bit of water. We'd thrown towels on the floor last night, so I threw those towels into the bathroom for now. But the bed . . . well, it was wet through.

I stripped the bedding and lifted the mattress, carrying

it out to the front deck.

Marit and Kari were clearly surprised, and Norah stood up. "Oh, what happened?"

"My bed got wet," I explained. "No big deal."

Marit cocked her head. "You wet the bed?" The language barrier wasn't embarrassing at all.

"No, no," I said, ignoring the grin on Paul's face. "Not wet like that. The tap and the valve in the bathroom . . ." I did the lever-hand action Marit did the other day so she'd understand. "It's no big deal."

"Oh, where will you sleep tonight?" Norah asked.

"Paul's got a spare bed. It's fine," I said dismissively, hoping they'd drop it.

By Marit and Kari's smirks, I think it might have been too late anyway.

"Breakfast is ready," Paul said a little too loudly. He gave me a 'please shut up' look before he turned his smile to his guests.

Breakfast was great. Back home, I'd have been lucky to choke down a coffee for breakfast on my way to work, but out here, getting up with the sun and having a full breakfast, then doing activities all day, outdoors in the fresh air . . . well, it was invigorating.

I felt like a different person.

Being with Paul and clearing away our pasts certainly had something to do with that. But being out here, surrounded by sunshine and wilderness . . . it was something I could get used to, that was for sure.

Paul said I needed a plan.

If we were going to move forward, I needed to figure out a sustainable way to do that.

To earn money, to pay my way, to help him.

If I wanted it bad enough, I'd find a way.

And I did want it. It was all I wanted.

"You okay?" Paul asked me quietly. We'd set off on our day of adventure, this time taking in Indigenous cave and rock art, and we were getting ready to hike in to the site. "You've been kinda quiet. At breakfast, on the drive out here."

I slid the backpack out of the back of the Cruiser. "Just thinking."

"About?"

"Making this happen," I said, lifting the full weight of his backpack. "Christ, this is heavy. Are you training for the Special Forces?"

He laughed. "Not quite."

"Here, turn around." I helped him put on the backpack. "Did you want me to take something out of here for you? I could halve your carry weight."

He shifted the bag on his back until he was comfortable. "Nah, I got it. I'm used to it now."

I mean, it certainly explained his physique. Hauling a twenty-five kilogram kit bag through the scrub, climbing over rocks and up and down rough terrain was no small feat.

I turned him around, not really giving him an option. I unclasped his backpack and took out the first aid kit and the top two insulated containers of food. It wasn't much, maybe five or six kilos at most. But surely it had to help.

"If I had a bigger backpack," I said, shoving them into my bag.

Paul tried to be annoyed but he relented a smile. "Thanks."

We began the hike in, Paul at the front, then Marit, Kari, and Norah, then me. It was getting warm, and this hike was all scrub. There were no overhead trees, no canopy for shade. We stopped a few times for water, and once Paul stopped, his hand up like a marine, and he pointed to his right.

There were two wallabies about twenty metres away. Marit and Kari were most excited, and they managed to snap some photos before the wallabies hopped away. Further along there was a huge goanna, maybe two metres long from its nose to the tip of its tail. Marit, Kari, and Norah were *not* excited to see that.

Paul put his arm out in a keep-back fashion, and we all sighed with relief when it sauntered off into the scrub.

It was so freaking awesome.

Better than my soul-sucking office job. Every day there was like purgatory, and I could kick myself for ever thinking Paul was crazy to want to do this.

I wondered if I could do it with him.

I wondered if he'd think that was a good idea.

Even if that was my Plan A, I'd still need a Plan B, C, and D.

I'd need contingencies to prove to him I was serious, that I'd thought it through. That I'd exhausted every possible option before I had to leave in two days.

Two days.

God. I wasn't ready to say goodbye again. Even if it wasn't permanent, even knowing I'd be seeing him again soon, it wasn't enough.

I didn't want to leave in two days.

The destination for the day was the site of some Indigenous rock art. There was a sheer rock face and trees that afforded some much-appreciated shade, an impressive overhang, a lookout, and a cave that was more of a slit in the ancient sandstone, all spotted with rock art. There were wooden paths to protect the ground, and the rock art itself was fenced off to stop people from trying to touch it.

It was sacred and beautiful and utterly amazing to think it was over tens of thousands of years old.

We took a moment to sit in the shade and take it all in. "It's peaceful here," I mused. Norah nodded, and Paul gave me a small, approving smile.

"It is. The First Nations people here, the Gundjeihmi-speaking people, call this place Burrunggui," Paul said. "And according to traditional owners, this was shaped by Ancestral beings in the creation period of the Dreaming. They would meet here, prepare food, and hold ceremonies. It holds a remarkable significance."

"I can see why."

It was true. There was a peacefulness here that was hard to explain.

Kari said something in Norwegian, and Marit translated for her. "She said it feels like the earth and the heart are happy here," Marit said.

I stared at her because that was exactly how it felt. I nodded, struggling to find my voice. "That's how it feels for me too."

I could feel Paul watching me, and when I was brave enough to meet his gaze, he smiled. A soft, private smile that cemented something in me.

Yeah.

I wasn't leaving in two days.

I WAS glad to get back into camp. The late afternoon was warm and humid, the view of the valley below shimmered in the rising heat. Clouds rolled in again for a late afternoon shower, a sure sign that summer was on its way.

It wasn't in the distance this time. It was right over us.

I managed to get my mattress back into my tent before the storm hit. I had no intention of sleeping on it, but I didn't want it to get ruined. Marit, Kari, and Norah were all in their tents, waiting for the rain to hit.

I made a run for the communal kitchen as the skies opened up, getting myself drenched in the dash.

I laughed, my arms outstretched, water dripping off me, my hair plastered down my forehead. "Holy shit. I feel like I walked out of the ocean."

Paul smirked and threw me a dishtowel to dry myself off with.

I shook my head like a dog and patted my face dry, and he was still looking at me, his eyes full of heat and desire.

"You should probably get out of those wet clothes," he said over the sound of the rain on the roof.

"Wanna help me with that?"

"Hell yes," he replied.

But a shriek of laughter came across the way and we turned to see Marit and Kari running into the rain, barefoot, still in their shorts and singlet tops. They laughed and danced, and then Norah pulled off her sandals and joined them.

I couldn't help but laugh, so I pulled off my shoes and socks. "Get your boots off," I said to Paul before I ran into the pouring rain. I was already wet, so it was no big deal.

But if I was ever going to have the chance to dance barefoot in the rain in the middle of Kakadu, I was going to take it.

I was surprised when Paul joined us. I didn't think he would. But he did. As barefoot and as soaking wet as the rest of us.

In the fading afternoon daylight, on the edge of the cliff overlooking the wetlands, we laughed and danced. Free, without a care in the world.

We probably looked mad, but it would be one of my fondest memories.

And afterward, when the rain cleared, we sat in the chairs overlooking the darkening world below us. Not talking, just taking it all in.

It had been a great day. One of the best days of my life, if I was being honest.

Because I'd made up my mind. I was staying here. I hadn't told Paul that yet. I hadn't worked out the finer details yet, but I had a plan brewing.

I just had to get him on board with it.

And from the way I'd caught him smiling at me a few times, the way it sent a rush of warmth right through me, the spark between us ready to ignite, I got the feeling he wouldn't mind.

CHAPTER SEVEN
PAUL

I'D TOLD MYSELF AND I'D TOLD DEREK THAT WE needed to *only talk*, knowing that falling back into bed, back into old habits, wouldn't be good for us.

But I was pretty sure I was going to blow that tonight.

Watching him laugh in the rain, the way his hair stuck to his forehead, around the nape of his neck, watching the happiness on his face . . .

There was no going back.

And we had talked. And we'd need to continue to communicate like we had been.

But tonight was going to end in orgasms.

I could feel it in my blood.

It had been a long day, full of long arduous hiking in warm and humid conditions, so I wasn't surprised when Norah called it a night early, and Marit and Kari soon followed.

Derek was washing up in the communal kitchen while I cleaned down the grill. I told him he didn't have to do that, but he just rolled his eyes and did it anyway. So I got busy scraping down the grill, and when I was done, I handed him the scraper to wash.

Everyone else was gone, the campsite dark. We were alone, and I risked a slow hand across his lower back.

"Thank you for helping me out today," I said.

He finished and pulled the plug. "You're welcome." He stayed where he was, turning his head. "Paul?"

"Yeah," I replied, standing close enough to feel his body heat.

"I'm not sleeping in my tent tonight," he whispered.

I smiled and dropped my forehead to his shoulder. "Good."

"And I know you said we should just talk, but—"

"I want you," I murmured. "Since I woke up next to you this morning. All day hiking. Seeing you at the rock art site, how you understood what the place meant. Then dancing in the rain. Derek—"

He turned then, his dark eyes pools of black fire. "Paul," he said, his voice rough. "Let's go."

He was gone so fast, I almost fell forward. But with a smile, I turned the kitchen light off and followed him into my cabin.

His shirt was already on the floor and he stopped with his shorts almost pulled down over his ass. His eyes caught mine. "Yes?"

"Fuck yes."

There was no stopping now. No reason or logic was going to convince my body to not do this. My blood was on fire, my balls were full and heavy, my cock already hard.

I hadn't had sex in so long.

I stood there, so mesmerised watching the magic of

him undressing, that I forgot about my own clothes. When he was fully naked, his long, lean body pale in the darkness, he smiled. "See something you like?"

I nodded, words failing me.

He chuckled and strode over to me, unbuttoning my shirt. "Oh," I said, beginning to help him.

He left the shirt for me and unbuttoned my shorts, groaning as he found out how hard I was. "Fuck, I've missed this," he said, palming me.

I hissed. "It's been a long time," I said. "I've not . . . since you . . ."

His nose was almost touching mine, his gaze intense. "Me either." He licked his lips. "I know we should probably work our way into familiar territory, start slow," he whispered. "But I really want you to fuck me. I want to remember. I want you inside me, where you belong."

My knees almost buckled. Then I remembered. *Fuck.* "I don't have anything . . ."

I wasn't kidding when I said I hadn't even looked at anyone since him.

He smirked and went to his bag. He pulled out a bottle of lube and threw it on the bed. I was confused. "I thought you said you hadn't . . ."

He bit his bottom lip. "I haven't had sex with anyone, but I jerk off a lot." He gave himself a long, slow pull, twisting his hand over the head of his cock.

Warmth pooled low in my belly and my cock twitched. "Get on the bed."

He grinned and, one knee at a time, slowly went to the middle of my bed. I threw him a towel, which he spread out, then he took his pillow and put it under his hips as he lay down.

So familiar, like we'd just done this yesterday. Like five years hadn't passed.

He stretched his back like a cat, perching his arse high in the air, and he began to jerk off. "I imagined this a thousand times," he whined. "Remembered every time, the feel of you inside me. Made me come every time."

I let out a puff of breath. I think I'd stopped breathing there for a minute. "Christ, Derek," I murmured. "This is going to be over before it begins."

He lifted his arse higher and smiled into the mattress. "Then stop wasting time."

I pulled off my briefs and crawled onto the bed behind him, running my hand over his arse and lower back. He moaned at the touch, arching his back even more, the hand on his cock working faster.

God, I was so hard already. This really was going to be over before it began.

I poured the lube down his crack, smearing his hole with my thumb, slipping it inside him. Gentle at first, slow and delicate. Then deeper and then another finger, until he whined at me. "Paul, I'm not fucking kidding."

I chuckled.

He hadn't changed one bit.

Still a greedy lover. Demanding, bossy.

With a hand on his shoulder, I pulled him up, so his back was to my chest, my cock pressed against his arse. He gasped, trying to back onto me. I held his hips still. "Are you sure you want me bare?"

We'd had condomless sex a thousand times. But that was before.

His chest was heaving. "You said you haven't been with anyone."

"I haven't. Not since you."

He groaned. "Then yes. Fuck me. Come inside me."

My cock pulsed at his words and he smirked, so I pushed him back down, his face into the mattress. And then I pushed my cock against his hole and slowly slipped inside him.

Hot and slick and so fucking tight.

"Holy shit," I breathed.

He whined, his fists now clawing the bed covers. "Oh fuck, yes."

I pushed all the way in, up to my balls. And I stayed there, letting him get used to it. He tried to push back, tried to make me move, so with my hand on his hip, I pressed into him. Deeper and harder to remind him who was in charge. He cried out, staying still then, breathing deep and measured.

After a few moments, when he was fully relaxed, he began to whine with each breath. Like he used to when he was truly ready for me to move.

We were so familiar, so in tune.

So I pulled out a little and slid back in a few times, and his hand went back to his cock. "Oh god, Paul. This is what I needed, so bad."

I put my hand on the bed by his shoulder and began to fuck him. Exactly how I knew he loved it, how he needed it.

He gasped with the change of angle, his hand moving fast, his hips rolling, and I was so deep inside him. He was so tight, taking me into his body like a glove. With his forehead pressed into the bed, he arched his back. "Paul, yes, right there, fuck," he groaned, his arse clenching tight around me as he came.

Milking me.

I thrust into him hard, once, twice, my cock rock hard and swollen, the coil of pleasure inside me winding tighter and tighter until it snapped.

My cock pulsed and spilled come deep inside him, and he gasped again, moaning as I filled him. The room spun, my world went white and fuzzy . . .

I'd never come so hard.

I'd never felt like this. Like all my wounds were healed, the pain of the past five years was gone. I collapsed on top of him, staying buried inside him, trying to catch my breath, to make sense of what my heart was trying to tell me.

I was home.

He was my home.

Eventually he moved, groaning as I rolled off him, but I quickly pulled him back into my arms. "Don't go too far," I murmured into the back of his head. "I'm not done with you yet."

He chuckled, sighing contentedly in my arms. Both of us dozed for a while, sleep swirling with happy thoughts and a happy heart.

Somewhere around 2:00 am, I woke him up with a sleepy trail of kisses over his chest. I rolled him onto his back, nestled myself between his legs, sucking on his nipples and flicking them with my tongue until he fisted my hair and wrapped his legs around me.

This time, I kissed him as I pushed into him. My tongue in his mouth with my cock in his arse, his legs around my waist, our fingers entwined. The slower I fucked him, the higher he lifted his legs, then his arms were around my neck, and we found our rhythm, like we always did.

Making love with Derek was so easy.

So right.

His eyes in the darkness, wide and vulnerable, pleading. All I could do was nod and kiss him deeper, giving him what he was silently asking for.

He whined and grunted, his head pushed back, neck corded, and his eyes rolled closed as I hit that magic spot inside him. He came with a silent scream, clawing at my back, and I followed him over the edge.

Coming inside him, making him mine all over again, was everything I needed.

When I cleaned him up, he could barely keep his eyes open, smiling and somewhat incoherent, like he was drunk on me. "Feel like yours again," he mumbled.

I grinned, my heart happy that he felt the same way. I tossed the washcloth toward my bathroom, wrapped my arms around him, then kissed the side of his head. "Because you are."

I closed my eyes, knowing morning would come all too soon.

He was only supposed to have one more day here, one more day with me.

We needed to change that.

We needed to discuss our futures. With him in my arms, it all seemed so simple. Yet I had to wonder what the morning light would bring.

He mumbled something into my chest that I didn't quite catch. "Mm, what did you say?"

"I don't want to go back," he murmured. "Stay here with you, forever."

I smiled into the dark, my arms tightening around him. It sounded so easy when he said it like that. "You make it sound so simple," I whispered, my heart thumping.

"'Cause it is. Now go to sleep. Busy day tomorrow."

I chuckled, rubbing his back.

Could it really be that simple?

CHAPTER EIGHT

DEREK

I woke up hot and sweaty until I realised I was clinging to Paul and he was the reason I was sweating before six o'clock in the morning.

I peeled my skin from his and rolled onto my back, earning myself a sharp ache in my arse. I smiled at the familiar reminder of what we'd done.

Sunlight was beginning to dawn outside, the last day of the tour. I was excited, sure. But more excited about my plan, about my future. And it had been a long time since I'd felt excited about anything.

I rolled out of bed and took a quick shower. I found myself grinning when I remembered the reason why my arse felt wet and slippery. The memory of Paul planting his seed in me burned in my chest, making my whole body tingle.

I couldn't remember feeling so alive.

I shut the water off, and as I grabbed for a towel, Paul walked in. "Morning," I said, still smiling.

He squinted one eye at me, his hair sticking up on one side. "Hm. You're awfully cheerful today."

"I have every reason to be."

Paul frowned. "It's your last day," he said.

I snorted. "No it's not." Then I looked down at his very naked body. Damn, he was so sexy. "Come on, hurry up and get showered, or I'll end up back in here with you, going for round three. I'll see if I can figure out the coffee."

I left him to it, getting dressed and going out to the communal kitchen. I had two brews made just as Paul joined me, right when the sun was coming up. I handed him his cup. "So," he began, eyeing me cautiously. "Want to explain the good mood?"

"I told you last night," I said, sipping my coffee. "Today's not my last day. I'm not leaving tomorrow. It's that simple." Then I shrugged. "I mean, there's more to it than that, and it's probably more complicated in the details, but the bottom line is I don't want to leave. I want to be with you. Not just living in Jabiru, like I thought could be a possibility." Jabiru was the closest town. It made sense, but it wasn't close enough. "But here, with you. At this camp. Helping you."

He stared at me.

"Come on, let's go sit out here," I said, walking to the chairs that faced the valley below.

I waited for him to join me.

"So that's your plan?" he asked.

I sighed contentedly, smiling as I sipped my coffee and taking in the glorious sunrise. "Yep."

"There are permit applications and some pretty strict rules that apply to working out here," he said. "It's not a simple procedure. It took weeks for mine to come through. They do background checks—"

"I'm fine with all that."

"They'll need valid reasons, economical reasons. My business does okay, Derek, but I don't know if it can sustain us both."

"I have a business plan," I said. "I can run additional astronomy tours. You can charge more. I can take them up to the ridge, or even just here. You can't tell me people wouldn't like that."

He opened his mouth, then he made a thoughtful face. "Um, maybe . . . ? I'd need to think on it. We'd need to run numbers and submit a changed business plan with the permit, and . . ." He shrugged and his eyes cut to mine. "It could work."

I grinned and settled back in the seat, gazing out across the wetlands as the sun rose. "If I get to do this during the day," I gestured out before us. "And you get to do me all night, then we will make this happen."

He chuckled, then sighed. "You're serious, yeah? You want this life? It's remote. It's new people every few days. It's tiring, it's subject to weather, and I've had some clients that are, how do I say it?"

"A pain in the arse."

"To put it mildly."

"I'm serious. I told you before, Paul. Whatever it takes. My place is here with you. Last night cemented that for me. I can't go back. My life in Darwin without you was killing me. I feel alive here."

"You said you'd thought about living in Jabiru?"

I nodded. Jabiru was a small town in Kakadu. There were houses, a fuel station, a fast-food place, and not much more. "I thought it could work, and if they knock back my application to work here with you, then I will look at Jabiru. Seeing you on weekends would be better than not at all."

Paul's eyes met mine, warm and filled with understanding. He got it now, just how serious I was.

"My place is with you," I said quietly. "When you strip away all the bullshit, it's really kinda simple. Whatever it takes."

He nodded. "We'll make it work."

"Yes, we will."

Norah's door opened and Paul stood up as she walked over. "Well, this looks nice," she said.

"Take a seat," Paul said. "I'll make a start on breakfast. Want a coffee?"

Then Marit and Kari joined us, and after breakfast, we loaded up the Cruiser and headed out. The last day was the biggest—a lot of hiking, a lot of driving—but it was by far the best day of the tour.

We were going to the Jim Jim Falls and finishing the tour with a sunset cruise on the Yellow River.

Getting to the waterfalls was an effort. A fair drive along the highway but then a very slow and bumpy drive along a dirt and sand road that ended at a carpark. From there we crossed a river on a punt, then hiked into the falls.

World famous, amazing, ancient, and breathtaking. They were worth the effort.

From the base of the falls, we hiked for a good ninety

minutes through the gorge to the private billabongs, which were like plunge pools carved from ancient stone.

It wasn't an easy hike, and I could see Paul kept his eye on Norah, but she was an absolute trooper. She was sweating and red-faced and puffing and panting. But she never once complained. She was first to her feet when we paused for a drink, and she loved every step.

She swam in the water, she mothered Marit and Kari, and me a little, if I was being honest. At first it was a bit weird, but over the last few days she'd really grown on me.

I offered her my hand when she had to jump down a long step on the way back to the Cruiser. Which I also offered to Kari and Marit as well, and then as a joke, I offered my hand to Paul. Marit and Kari giggled, and from the way they looked between me and Paul, I was sure they knew something was going on between us.

It did make me wonder what we'd do, down the track, if my business proposal became a reality and we ran these tours as a couple.

Would we keep sharing his cabin?

Would we even be a *couple* when we had clients?

I couldn't take a tent for myself, because then we'd be cutting into how many clients we could manage. But maybe some clients wouldn't want to be stuck out in the middle of nowhere with a gay couple.

"What are you quiet for?" Marit asked in the Cruiser on the way to the Yellow River cruise. It was now late afternoon, it'd been a long day already, and those hours of missed sleep were now catching up with me. Plus, my mind was running through a hundred scenarios. "You look worried."

I didn't miss the flash of Paul's eyes in the rear-view mirror. "I'm not worried," I said, offering a smile I didn't quite rightly feel.

"You don't want to leave tomorrow," she said. "We don't want to leave either. But we fly from Darwin tomorrow night."

"I'm not leaving tomorrow," I said, trying the words out for size. It felt good. All eyes turned to me, including Paul's in the rear-view. "I have a few extra days. Part of a new stargazer tour that Paul's trialling."

"Oh, with your telescope?" Marit asked excitedly. "Oh, so amazing."

"Is it new?" Norah asked. "I'd have liked to have gone on that."

I smiled at Paul in his reflection. "Yeah, it's only new. Still in the trial phase. But you all enjoyed the stargazing we did."

They all agreed with enthusiastic nods. "Very much," Kari said.

It was probably silly, being a very small test group of sorts. But it bolstered me to think my plan could actually work. The hope that seeded in my chest was growing into something more like determination. People travelled from all over to see the stars from Kakadu. My plan could actually work.

Would it be easy? No.

Would we need to work out how we lived, worked, and coexisted as a couple? Sure.

But it *was* possible.

THE SUNSET CRUISE WAS MAGICAL. Birds, crocodiles, even wild horses, and a sunset like only Kakadu could do made an excellent end to a great little tour.

It was the perfect end to four perfect days.

Four days that righted wrongs and gave me back my life.

When we got back to camp, I was almost sorry there was no late-night storm that made us take shelter in our tents. While part of me was bummed that I didn't get Paul to myself, part of me was happy to sit around on the camp chairs and talk.

Marit and Kari were flying back to Norway, and Norah had two days in Darwin before heading back to Sydney.

"So when do you go back to Darwin?" Norah asked me. "How long does your stargazing thing go for?"

"Unsure at this point," I said vaguely. "Hoping for it to be a permanent thing."

"It'd be an amazing experience," Norah said. "I feel very privileged to see what you showed me. Not many other people can say they saw Saturn from Kakadu."

It made me happy to hear her say that. "Should I get my telescope out?"

"Oh yes, please," she said. Marit and Kari also agreed.

So we spent another hour or two looking skyward. I showed them constellations and planets. The way Paul smiled at me made me proud.

And when it was too late and no one could withhold yawns, we said goodnight. I went straight into Paul's cabin, kicked off my shoes, pulled off my shirt, and fell onto the bed.

It had been a long day.

"I'm tired," I murmured as Paul came in.

He pulled off his boots and sighed as he crawled onto the bed, over my body. He kissed up my stomach. "You were great today," he said, kissing a slow path up to my chest. "I could get used to having you here, helping me."

I carded my fingers through his short hair and pulled his head up so he was looking at me. "You'll have to get used to it. Because I'm not leaving."

"You'll have to go back at some point," he said. "To get your things, to finalise paperwork, your apartment."

"But not for long. A few days, at most." I sighed. "I was thinking today . . . How will it work? How will we be us and run your business? Will your clients know we're together? Will they boycott you because of that? Paul, I don't want to jeopardise what you've worked so hard for."

His eyes met mine. "Where did your confidence go? That adamant 'I'm not leaving' line you said half a minute ago?"

"I'm not leaving . . . I don't want to leave. But this is a reality question. It's a 'how do we move forward' question."

He smiled. "We'll work it out. I've never hidden who I am, and I don't expect to start now. We can just tell folks that this cabin has two single beds."

"But it doesn't."

"They don't know that." He kissed my lips. "But I like that you're thinking of these things. You're thinking about reality."

"I'm trying. I won't always get it right, Paul. But I'm trying."

"I know you are." He kissed my sternum, then kissed

the tattoo over my heart. He stared at it, then rolled us onto our sides, collected me in his arms, and brushed my hair off my forehead. He searched my eyes and traced his finger down my lips, chin, to my chest, and back to the tattoo. "You said this nebula is like you. Because it decimates everything in its path."

I knew he'd bring that up eventually. I didn't really want to talk about it, but if I was going to learn how to be honest with him, it started now.

"It's how I felt when you left," I admitted. "That I'd taken your love and decimated it. I'd ruined everything good in my life. Everything that was pure and worth anything. Until there was nothing left, just a massive black hole."

He smiled sadly. "No, this nebula is like you because it's made up of a million beautiful moving parts just looking for peace."

Oh god.

"You search the sky every night looking for peace, but, Derek, it's not up there. It's right here," he said, his palm pressed over my heart. "The peace you need to look for is in here."

I nodded, because I knew that was true. It just hurt. "My peace starts here with you."

He smiled, tired and heavy lidded. He kissed me, soft and warm. "Too tired to get up," he mumbled.

Washing faces and brushing teeth could wait. I pulled him closer and rested my chin against the side of his face and smiled into the darkness.

My peace started here.

My peace had already started.

EPILOGUE
PAUL

EIGHTEEN MONTHS LATER

I JUMPED OUT OF THE CRUISER, HANDED ONE BOX of supplies to Derek, grabbed the other, and we dashed into the communal kitchen.

"He's on his way now," I said over the sound of the wind.

"He's insane," Derek said, looking out at the storm about to hit. "This one's gonna be a doozy."

I nodded. "Sure is." The air was already charged, thunder rolled overhead, and cracks of lightning lit up the too-dark afternoon sky. "Did you get the tie-downs done?"

"Yep. She's all secure as it can be." Derek was stacking the supplies into the fridge and cupboards. "Tent two stuck a bit. Thought I was gonna have to wait for you, but I got it in."

When storms like this hit, we needed to make sure our

whole campsite was locked down and secure. We couldn't afford damaged tents or, worse still, someone getting injured.

Having Derek here was a godsend. In the beginning, I'd worried about how it'd all work, with money and getting his stargazing tours up and running, but it had been incredible. And he never stopped working. He was either mowing grass, clipping the trees around the campsite, making everything more client-friendly without losing any of the natural charm. He taught himself how to sew canvas patches on the eco canopies on the tents, he cooked meals, he cleaned up. He made my tours run more smoothly, taking half my workload without complaint. And once a month, he ran his own night-time astronomy tours. Which were booked solid. We were considering maybe introducing more throughout the year.

It hadn't been all smooth sailing. We'd had some adjustment issues and a few arguments, but mostly it had been the best personal and professional decision I'd ever made.

But he, himself, the Derek I used to know—the moody and brooding Derek, the Derek that would sometimes let the darkness in—was gone. Sure, he was still a little moody sometimes, but taking him out of his old life, where his past was only ever a step behind him, had been good for him.

Being outdoors was good for him.

Being surrounded by this remote and rugged country was good for him.

Being able to watch and study the stars whenever he wanted was good for him.

Being here with me was good for him.

He was good for me too.

With the last of the supplies put away, I took his face in my hands and kissed him. "What was that for?" he asked with a smile.

"Thank you," I said. "For being here. For being great. I love you."

He grinned, his long hair tousled by the wind. "I love you too."

"You know what we should do?" I asked. The wind stopped as though it was listening to us and wanted to hear my answer. But then the rain dropped, fat and heavy drops in a deluge. A crack of thunder boomed right above us.

We both ducked on instinct and laughed. "Holy shit!" he yelled over the roar of the storm. "What should we do?"

Leaning in, I still had to yell so he could hear me. "We should fuck all afternoon."

He looked at me, wide eyed, and he laughed. "Oh really?"

I nodded and gestured to the empty tents. "No guests today."

Just then, the old Jeep pulled up. "What were you saying?" Derek asked.

I waved him off. "Tully doesn't count."

"Pretty sure he does."

Tully Larson was the storm chaser who would use our camp as a base intermittently during the height of the electrical storm season. He had another camp further up toward the coast, still in Kakadu, but access was tough going in the wet season. He'd arrive here, say hello, maybe stay a night or two to wait for the perfect storm, then disappear into the wilderness for days on end.

Only this time, he was bringing someone.

His guest was a meteorologist from Melbourne, apparently. A fulminologist, to be exact. If you'd ever heard of such a thing. Someone who studies lightning.

Tully ran into the communal kitchen area, unfazed by the rain, his grin wide. His blond shaggy hair stuck to his head, his shirt clung to his chest, but he didn't seem to care. He was a storm chaser after all. Rain was nothing to him.

"G'day fellas," he said, shaking my hand, then Derek's. "Real good to see ya's again."

Another man appeared then, just as wet but clearly more bothered. He was dripping water from his short dark hair, he had stunning dark blue eyes, and a frown. He was also wearing proper shorts and a button-down shirt and boots; his outfit screamed scientist on a field trip, but at least he wore boots.

God, he had the bluest eyes I'd ever seen.

"This is Jeremiah," Tully said. "Jeremiah, this is Paul and Derek. They run this place. And they live here."

"You live here?" Jeremiah asked. Stunned. Horrified. "All the way out here?"

I laughed and gestured to the wall of water that was rain just a few feet away. "Best address on the planet. But," I pointed to our cabin, "more specifically, that's our home right there. Tully will look after you tonight, but if there's an emergency, you come find us."

Then I clapped Tully on the shoulder. "I put you guys in tent one. Fridge is full. You know where everything is.

We're gonna be busy for a few hours. If you need us for anything, you don't need us for anything." I winked. "If you know what I mean."

He grinned. "Loud and clear."

Derek and I made a quick run for our cabin. He locked the door, and I grabbed us a towel each before we stripped out of our wet clothes. "I can't believe you told him that," Derek said.

I laughed. "Remember when you thought me and the storm guy were a thing?"

Derek rolled his eyes as he dried himself. "That was before I ever met him. He's cute, in a Patrick Swayze from *Point Break* kinda way, but he's not your type. I know that now."

"Oh really? What's my type?"

He threw his towel onto the bed, standing before me stark naked. "Me. I'm your type."

"Yes, you are." I gave him a few strokes while I kissed down his neck, then I captured his mouth with mine. "Now get on the bed."

Thunder boomed overhead and lightning lit up the sky outside. The air between us crackled, charged with energy. Derek smirked and did as I told him. As the summer storm wreaked havoc outside, we made slow love, over and over. Steamy and sweaty, our bodies joining in the most inti-mate of ways, the way our hearts already had.

As one, and forever.

THE STORM BOYS SERIES

Want to read Tully and Jeremiah's story?

Outrun the Rain
Into the Tempest
Touch the Lightning

THE STORM BOYS SERIES

ABOUT THE AUTHOR

N.R. Walker is an Australian author, who loves her genre of gay romance. She loves writing and spends far too much time doing it, but wouldn't have it any other way.

She is many things: a mother, a wife, a sister, a writer. She has pretty, pretty boys who live in her head, who don't let her sleep at night unless she gives them life with words.

She likes it when they do dirty, dirty things... but likes it even more when they fall in love.

She used to think having people in her head talking to her was weird, until one day she happened across other writers who told her it was normal.

She's been writing ever since...

ALSO BY N.R. WALKER

Blind Faith

Through These Eyes (Blind Faith #2)

Blindside: Mark's Story (Blind Faith #3)

Ten in the Bin

Gay Sex Club Stories 1

Gay Sex Club Stories 2

Point of No Return – Turning Point #1

Breaking Point – Turning Point #2

Starting Point – Turning Point #3

Element of Retrofit – Thomas Elkin Series #1

Clarity of Lines – Thomas Elkin Series #2

Sense of Place – Thomas Elkin Series #3

Taxes and TARDIS

Three's Company

Red Dirt Heart

Red Dirt Heart 2

Red Dirt Heart 3

Red Dirt Heart 4

Red Dirt Christmas

Cronin's Key

Cronin's Key II

Cronin's Key III

Cronin's Key IV - Kennard's Story

Exchange of Hearts

The Spencer Cohen Series, Book One

The Spencer Cohen Series, Book Two

The Spencer Cohen Series, Book Three

The Spencer Cohen Series, Yanni's Story

Blood & Milk

The Weight Of It All

A Very Henry Christmas (The Weight of It All 1.5)

Perfect Catch

Switched

Imago

Imagines

Imagoes

Red Dirt Heart Imago

On Davis Row

Finders Keepers

Evolved

Galaxies and Oceans

Private Charter

Nova Praetorian

A Soldier's Wish

Upside Down

The Hate You Drink

Sir

Tallowwood

Reindeer Games

The Dichotomy of Angels

Throwing Hearts

Pieces of You - Missing Pieces #1

Pieces of Me - Missing Pieces #2

Pieces of Us - Missing Pieces #3

Lacuna

Tic-Tac-Mistletoe

Bossy

Code Red

Dearest Milton James

Dearest Malachi Keogh

Christmas Wish List

Code Blue

Davo

The Kite

Learning Curve

Merry Christmas Cupid

To the Moon and Back

TITLES IN AUDIO:

Cronin's Key

Cronin's Key II

Merry Christmas Cupid

To the Moon and Back

SERIES COLLECTIONS:

Red Dirt Heart Series

Turning Point Series

Thomas Elkin Series

Spencer Cohen Series

Imago Series

Blind Faith Series

FREE READS:

Sixty Five Hours

Learning to Feel

His Grandfather's Watch (And The Story of Billy and Hale)

The Twelfth of Never (Blind Faith 3.5)

Twelve Days of Christmas (Sixty Five Hours Christmas)

Best of Both Worlds

TRANSLATED TITLES:

ITALIAN

Fiducia Cieca (Blind Faith)

Attraverso Questi Occhi (Through These Eyes)

Preso alla Sprovvista (Blindside)

Il giorno del Mai (Blind Faith 3.5)

Cuore di Terra Rossa Serie (Red Dirt Heart Series)

Natale di terra rossa (Red dirt Christmas)

Intervento di Retrofit (Elements of Retrofit)

A Chiare Linee (Clarity of Lines)

Senso D'appartenenza (Sense of Place)

Spencer Cohen Serie (including Yanni's Story)

Punto di non Ritorno (Point of No Return)

Punto di Rottura (Breaking Point)

Punto di Partenza (Starting Point)

Imago (Imago)

Imagines

Il desiderio di un soldato (A Soldier's Wish)

Scambiato (Switched)

Tallowwood

The Hate You Drink

Ho trovato te (Finders Keepers)

Cuori d'argilla (Throwing Hearts)

Galassie e Oceani (Galaxies and Oceans)

Il peso di tut (The Weight of it All)

FRENCH

Confiance Aveugle (Blind Faith)

A travers ces yeux: Confiance Aveugle 2 (Through These Eyes)

Aveugle: Confiance Aveugle 3 (Blindside)

À Jamais (Blind Faith 3.5)

Cronin's Key Series

Au Coeur de Sutton Station (Red Dirt Heart)

Partir ou rester (Red Dirt Heart 2)

Faire Face (Red Dirt Heart 3)

Trouver sa Place (Red Dirt Heart 4)

Le Poids de Sentiments (The Weight of It All)

Un Noël à la sauce Henry (A Very Henry Christmas)

Une vie à Refaire (Switched)

Evolution (Evolved)

Galaxies & Océans

Qui Trouve, Garde (Finders Keepers)

Sens Dessus Dessous (Upside Down)

La Haine au Fond du Verre (The hate You Drink)

Tallowwood

Spencer Cohen Series

GERMAN

Flammende Erde (Red Dirt Heart)

Lodernde Erde (Red Dirt Heart 2)

Sengende Erde (Red Dirt Heart 3)

Ungezähmte Erde (Red Dirt Heart 4)

Vier Pfoten und ein bisschen Zufall (Finders Keepers)

Ein Kleines bisschen Versuchung (The Weight of It All)

Ein Kleines Bisschen Fur Immer (A Very Henry Christmas)

Weil Leibe uns immer Bliebt (Switched)

Drei Herzen eine Leibe (Three's Company)

Über uns die Sterne, zwischen uns die Liebe (Galaxies and Oceans)

Unnahbares Herz (Blind Faith 1)

Sehendes Herz (Blind Faith 2)

Hoffnungsvolles Herz (Blind Faith 3)

Verträumtes Herz (Blind Faith 3.5)

Thomas Elkin: Verlangen in neuem Design

Thomas Elkin: Leidenschaft in klaren

Thomas Elkin: Vertrauen in bester Lage

Traummann töpfern leicht gemacht (Throwing Hearts)

Sir

THAI

Sixty Five Hours (Thai translation)

Finders Keepers (Thai translation)

SPANISH

Sesenta y Cinco Horas (Sixty Five Hours)

Los Doce Días de Navidad

Código Rojo (Code Red)

Código Azul (Code Blue)

Queridísimo Milton James

Queridísimo Malachi Keogh

El Peso de Todo (The Weight of it All)

Tres Muérdagos en Raya: Serie Navidad en Hartbridge

Lista De Deseos Navideños: Serie Navidad en Hartbridge

Feliz Navidad Cupido: Serie Navidad en Hartbridge

Spencer Cohen Libro Uno

Spencer Cohen Libro Dos

Spencer Cohen Libro Tres

Davo

Hasta la Luna y de Vuelta

CHINESE

Blind Faith

JAPANESE

Bossy

Ingram Content Group UK Ltd.
Milton Keynes UK
UKHW040801300523
422560UK00001B/9